Love is
a time of enchantment:
in it all days are fair and all fields
green. Youth is blest by it,
old age made benign:
the eyes of love see
roses blooming in December,
and sunshine through rain. Verily
is the time of true-love
a time of enchantment — and
Oh! how eager is woman
to be bewitched!

THE EAGLE'S PAWN

During the turbulent era of the Napoleonic Wars, young Caroline Fielding joins the household of General Sir Edmund Franklyn and his family. Intrigue, espionage, and the strong interplay of personal relationships await her there. Two men court her, and the Duke of Wellington enters her sphere as the British forces advance towards the Battle of Waterloo. In a thrilling climax many mysteries are elucidated, and Caroline discovers her final destiny in a true and lasting relationship with the man she loves.

Books by Clare Frances Holmes
in the Ulverscroft Large Print Series

SEASON OF INNOCENCE
THE IMPERIAL STAR

CLARE FRANCES HOLMES

THE EAGLE'S PAWN

Complete and Unabridged

ULVERSCROFT
Leicester

First published in Great Britain

First Large Print Edition
published September 1994

British Library CIP Data

Holmes, Clare Frances
The eagle's pawn.—Large print ed.—
Ulverscroft large print series: romance
I. Title
823.914 [F]

ISBN 0-7089-3147-2

Published by
F. A. Thorpe (Publishing) Ltd.
Anstey, Leicestershire

Set by Words & Graphics Ltd.
Anstey, Leicestershire
Printed and bound in Great Britain by
T. J. Press (Padstow) Ltd., Padstow, Cornwall

This book is printed on acid-free paper

1

WE were very happy together, in Oxford, my father and I. He was professor of languages at St Botolph's College; and my earliest recollections are of seeing the students scurrying across the quad on their way to their lectures; of handling the leather bindings of the books my father used; and of hearing the mellifluous bells of Oxford chiming at all hours.

I was born in 1792. My mother died three years later, and her place had been taken and our household ruled by my Aunt Betsey, a capable lady of kindly heart but formidable mien. We lived in the Professor's Lodging, within the quad, so that we were always a part of the College and its activities. My earliest years were spent within the shadow of Oxford's ancient walls.

My father was abstracted and immersed in his work. I was left largely to my own devices, though I remember that I received the beginnings of my education at a dame school in Scuttle Lane, off The High. It was inevitable, I suppose, that I should be drawn into the main purpose of The Professor's Lodging: the teaching of languages, both ancient and present-day. My activities were soon noted by Aunt Betsey, and received her disapproval.

"It's not right, Stephen," she scolded my father. "You have that child every spare hour with her nose and eyes in books. She should be attending to other matters, to befit her for her adult life. What good will Latin and French do her, may I ask, when the time comes and she wishes to become betrothed?"

"You are precipitating events, Betsey," my father answered mildly. "Caroline is only twelve. Besides, I thought she was already well-versed in womanly matters. You told me yourself that she can bake, turn sheets and clean windows. Indeed, I have remarked her efforts in The Lodgings. Surely you can allow her a little recreation?"

That the learning of irregular French verbs and Spanish syntax was a form of pleasure to my father, was clear to see. And it was a pleasure to me to be in my father's company, and earn his praise. But I sought to please my Aunt Betsey too, knowing of her stalwart efforts for us. In my spare time, I recall, I worked her a sampler and hung the finished picture over her bed.

It was to be expected that, as I grew up a little, I should become friends with some of the students. They made much of me, treating me as a younger sister; bringing me small presents and writing to me during the long vacation. But one student stood above all others, to my mind. Gérard, a young Frenchman from Paris, was my favourite. He epitomised to me all the students' most endearing traits; he was gay, carefree, serious, kindly and devil-may-care.

My father was criticised for Gérard's presence in the college. "Is it wise, Professor Lancing, to entertain within your college a Frenchman?" the Master of the University asked my father. "You know that since the rise of Napoleon Bonaparte, French ways and customs are frowned on by the authorities. The French are our enemies. I question the correctness of your conduct in teaching this Parisian. I must consider whether or not to ask this foreigner to leave."

"But surely the bounds of scholarship transcend those of nationality and expediency," my father had replied. "Gérard is a model pupil. Perhaps he will return to France to tell his compatriots of our way of life. His visit here and his return to France may aid the way to peace. And surely that is what all people in England now strongly desire."

"I approve of your sentiments," the Master had answered austerely. "But not the means of their expression. There can be no peace between England and France while Napoleon Bonaparte lives."

Gérard knew that his studies were now under a cloud. He came to see my father and myself often, as if he knew he must soon be banished. It was as if he had gained some maturity and sense of purpose during his days at St Botolph's College, and he wished us to know this, and to assure us of his regard.

I was now fourteen, and could better appreciate the unusual character of the young Frenchman. In any gathering he stood out; he was often the focal point of college discussions and activities. I admired his appearance, too. He was stocky in build with a pale complexion and auburn hair. He was always well dressed, as if his family had money; yet he was entirely natural in his behaviour. He clearly had qualities all his own.

We walked sometimes beside the Isis, admiring the fronds of the weeping-willows reflected in the water; seeing the Oxford bridges tremulously mirrored in the river. He talked to me much, and I enjoyed hearing his views and conclusions. Just before he disappeared, he said:

"Do not be afraid of life, Caroline. But instead, give yourself to life, as if granting to life a gift."

He paused, as if considering whether to amplify his statement, and say more. He continued, "To have cause, a purpose in life, is the only way to find your own talents and inner purposes. Without this conviction," — and he waved his arm towards the buildings of the University — "all the learning of Oxford is but a shallow thing, and in vain."

I pondered his words, but could not glimpse their intended purpose. I remember I looked at him questioningly, but Gérard stood suddenly still as if I were forgotten and he was miles away.

He took me back to the Lodgings, and stayed for our simple meal. Afterwards, he went to his room, and then returned to me as I sat sewing in a window-seat of the study.

"I have brought you this," he said. It was a pressed rose. "I preserved this flower within my translation of Ovid, on the day I met you. And now I wish you to have it. Please remember me. I doubt that we shall ever meet again."

The next day, he had gone. All his dues and fees were paid in full, and he left for my father a beautiful volume of Aristophanes' plays. The college seemed emptier by his going; and for a time, my studies were pursued without zeal.

Gérard was my first and strongest attachment made in Oxford. I mourned his going, as if he were dead. I did not know how vital a part this friendship was to play in my future life.

★ ★ ★

At this time the whole of England was threatened with invasion by Napoleon. "That dratted man," Aunt Betsey said. "He will not rest until he tries to land on English shores. He seems invincible. Everything falls into his grasp. Soon, only England will stand against him. He is a tyrant. An ogre. God had forgotten mercy when that man was formed."

My father was more explicit. "The Czar of Russia has recognised Napoleon's conquests in Europe. And Napoleon has granted the Czar leave to extend Russia's frontiers to include Finland. Yes, it is true, Caroline, Napoleon will seek to invade. We must all be ready for the day, and acquit ourselves as best we can."

Napoleon was the bogeyman of Europe. Naughty children were threatened by his name. But the fear was real. Beacons were laid on cliff-tops, ready to be lit when the French fleet was sighted. Our troops were kept on the alert; volunteers were trained and ready. The women of England were exhorted to defy the invader, while their children burned effigies of the Corsican.

7

And still he continued his triumphant course.

In 1808, when I was sixteen, an event occurred which changed for ever the course of my life. My father, Stephen Lancing, passed away.

He came into our sitting-room one afternoon, during an interval from his tutorial, and I made him a dish of tea. He sat quietly beside the centre table of our room which was piled high, as always, with his books. I remember he laid his hand upon his books, and I saw with surprise that his hand trembled.

"What is the matter, Father?" I asked. "Have you caught cold. Is it a chill?"

"I am a little weary," he replied, and he turned his fine blue eyes to me, and a smile lit his lined, aquiline face. He suddenly removed his wig; a thing I had never seen him do before. I saw that his hair was brown still, and curled slightly, even after the pressure of the curled, grey hair-piece.

"Have I never told you, you are growing up to be like your mother, Caroline?" he said to me gently. "I must make some arrangements for you.

8

It is no life for a young lady to be shut up in an Oxford college with students and savants. You should make some kind of debut into society. I am sorry I seem so ill equipped to prepare you for adult life.

"See, this is a miniature of your mother," he resumed. "Keep it always. She had great hopes for you. Hopes she did not live to see fulfilled. And now I . . ."

"Aunt Betsey, Aunt Betsey," I cried, for a sudden fear and consternation filled me. Aunt Betsey entered, and saw at once that my father was desperately ill. She sent me for the doctor while she prepared my father for bed. But even as we, together, helped him into his bed, in the room overlooking the quad, he turned to me and pressed my hand, and quietly passed away from this life.

His going had been so sudden and unexpected, I felt as if a catastrophe of nature had occurred. At his funeral service the whole University of Oxford assembled, and the Master read the lesson and gave the valedictory address. My father's students from St Botolph's lined his way, and twelve of them carried his bier. The choir of St Mary the Virgin sang his favourite anthems; and the perpetual bells of Oxford chimed his farewell, as they had, for so many years, chimed his earthly days and nights.

During the whole of that night and the following day my father's students of St Botolph's stood in the Great Hall of the college, and in turn, by rota, recited his translations of the Greek and Latin poets and philosophers.

I attempted to attend, sitting on a chair the students had brought in for me especially. But the solemnity and the poignancy of the occasion was too much for me. I left, seeking the arms of Aunt Betsey, where I shared her woe. It was only the pressing necessity of our future that finally brought us out of our sorrowing, and made us face our predicament, and our future.

"The Master of St Luke's College has offered me the post of housekeeper," Aunt Betsey told me. "There is a small room there for you, Caroline. I made that a condition. You must seek some occupation for yourself, dear child. But at least, this room with myself will be a

10

base for you. Somewhere that you can think of as home."

What could I do? I was sixteen, of average education, and with proficiency in Latin, French and Spanish. Who would want such a person? I asked myself. What could my future be? And I was not attractive, I told myself. Or even prepossessing. Looks had not mattered in our lives at St Botolph's. My hair had no curls. My lips no shine. The future looked bleak, and my ability to meet it seemed nonexistent.

"Your father told me sometime ago, that in the event of his death I must at once communicate with an old friend of his. A gentleman with whom he was himself a student at Oxford, and with whom he made a pact of mutual help.

"This gentleman is named . . . Let me find the paper . . . Sir Edmund Franklyn. He is I think a Colonel in the Dragoons, and is stationed at . . . Let me see . . . Lyddford Barracks, in Kent.

"I will write to him forthwith and we will await his reply. At the very least, he can give us advice, and may know of someone who may require a governess.

11

Yes, that would suit you, Caroline!

"You could become governess to a nice young girl, or a small family. They might even require Latin! You never know. And that sampler you embroidered for me is beautiful. You could offer any employer all round skills, my dear . . . "

Aunt Betsey was running on to prevent herself from weeping. I tried to steel myself, but the sight of my poor Aunt's distress was too much for me. I held her rotund figure in my arms, and dried her eyes. I knew how much I loved her homely, scolding ways; her figure had become stout, her hair grey, her eyes rheummy in the caring of my father and myself.

When our fit of grief was over, we busied ourselves clearing the Professor's Lodging, and taking my aunts possessions over to her new home in St Luke's. She herself carried the sampler, and hung it over her new bed. Her room was smaller than that at St Botolph's, and the room designated for myself was little better than a cupboard. But we put as cheerful a face on things as we could, and arranged our possessions. It seemed to both of us that

12

our parting was not far distant.

Within a few days, a reply was received from General Sir Edmund Franklyn. He was deeply distressed, he wrote, to hear of the passing of his old friend, Stephen Lancing, and would do all in his power to fulfil his obligation of assistance to Miss Caroline.

It so happened, the General wrote, that Lady Franklyn was a semi-invalid, and was herself in need of a companion, to help her pass the hours when she was confined to bed.

Lady Franklyn's interests were literary and artistic, and she required someone to read to her from the classics, and to discuss the matter read. A knowledge of French would particularly be welcome as Lady Franklyn admired the French poets, and wrote a little poetry herself. Also, Miss Caroline would be required to perform personal errands, and generally attend to Lady Franklyn's comfort.

The matter of remuneration was mentioned, and a period of trial suggested. Sir Edmund requested that if possible Miss Caroline should come to Charlecote Manor as soon as possible, and he proposed that his carriage should come to Oxford on the following day to convey Miss Caroline to her new post. He remained . . . Our obedient servant . . . Edmund Franklyn.

At once, we were thrown into consternation. Aunt Betsey packed my meagre selection of clothing in an old leather case which had once held a dozen lexicons. She made some attempt to crimp my hair, but the tresses remained obstinately straight. She pinched my cheeks, but no colour came. She found a bonnet which The Master's wife had discarded, but it fell over my eyes. We gave up trying to alter my normal appearance. "After all, dear," Aunt Betsey said. "It is not looks, but character that counts."

On the following day at the appointed time, a carriage drew up at the entrance to the quadrangle. I saw to my surprise that this was no ordinary carriage, but was clearly a vehicle with military connections. The arms of the 18th Dragoons were painted upon the door; and one trooper held the reins while another sat astride the piebald horse.

I had told no one of my departure, so I was greatly surprised to see so many of my father's students congregating in the quad as the carriage awaited me. They pressed around me as I walked to the carriage, calling my name, their good wishes, asking for letters, holding towards me their gifts of books. Many small posies were pressed into my hands as the trooper opened the carriage-door.

The students surrounded the carriage at first, and would not allow the troopers on their way. The troopers took the delay in good part. Then the horses became restive, and the driver cracked his whip. With the students' farewell cries still in my ears the horses pressed forward and the carriage sped swiftly away.

I had with me three sovereigns in a silk purse; the leather case containing my clothes, the miniature of my mother, the pressed rose from Gérard, and a wicker basket filled with books. I had been careful to include a French, Latin and Spanish dictionary. And so I set out to face my new life.

2

IT was now Spring in this year of 1808, but the weather was still cold, and the landscape as we passed was but filmed with the greenery of grasses and leaves. The clouds of the sky rode high above us as the carriage made its way out of Oxford, and tackled the southern roadways into Kent.

A mood of anxiety and depression now assailed me. What would my new employers be like? Had Sir Edmund Franklyn offered to me this post to fulfil his youthful obligation to my father as a formality only? Would he and Lady Franklyn soon dismiss me, on a pretext, yet retain the satisfaction of having fulfilled a promise made in the heady days of youth? The family sounded intimidating. Their titles oppressed me. I looked at the sturdy back of the trooper as he drove the coach, at the competent movements of the trooper who rode astride the leading horse. At least they

16

were strong, dependable men and from their presence I drew an intangible and wry kind of reassurance and comfort.

After some time of journeying we reached a town. It was clear that this was in the military occupation of a regiment of cavalry. Gun-carriages and military vehicles were being manouvered by horse power through the streets. Dragoons of the 18th Regiment were moving smartly, in formation, about their occasions.

I plucked up my courage, and spoke to the driver. "What is the name of this town, if you please?" I asked him. He turned his head.

"This is Lyddford, Miss. The barrack town and camp-site of the 18th Dragoons. Sir Edmund is their commanding officer, and he is highly respected by all ranks. You will find him fair and approachable, Miss."

"Thank you. There is great activity here. Is there warning of the invasion?"

"Invasion is a constant threat, Miss. The Dragoons are on a twenty-four hour alert. If our testing-time comes, the county of Kent will not find us wanting."

I am sure of it, I thought. Then other things occupied my mind, as the carriage began to approach Charlecote Manor.

The Manor lay a few miles outside Lyddford, yet its approach was screened by trees, and its site was hidden and private. I saw at first only tall walls topped with fronds of ivy, and a huge iron gate. Then the carriage had entered the drive and I saw the house before me.

The original edifice had been built in Queen Anne style, but later additions had been built on, so that the gracious old place sprawled before us, a structure of mellowed red brick, white paint, and gleaming windows. Somehow, the appearance of the house reassured me. I could not imagine that anyone of a mean disposition could live in and care for such a friendly old house.

The trooper brought down my luggage, and rang the bell for me. After a moment the big door opened, and a tall and angular woman in black dress and white mob cap and apron stood before me.

"Miss Caroline Lancing?" she enquired with a smile. "Please to enter. I am Mrs

Bagehot, the housekeeper. Lady Deborah is expecting you."

I stepped inside the polished hall, with its panelling, its oriental rugs, its oil-painted pictures, and stood, awaiting directions. It was at this moment that a door at the end of the hallway opened, and a man entered the broad corridor. He smiled when he saw me, and advanced towards Mrs Bagehot and myself.

"You must be Caroline Lancing," he said. "I am Philip Hellier, Sir Edmund's nephew. Welcome to Charlecote. I trust your stay here will be a happy one."

And Philip Hellier took my hand in his with a formal salute, while my breath was caught in my throat, and my heart thudded against the stays of my dress.

* * *

I saw that Philip Hellier was tall, well-built though not fleshy. The colour of his face was high, but not ruddy; his eyes were blue, a little prominent, his mouth well formed. His hair was fair on the top, yet undercut with brown. The whole was an effect of handsome and confident masculinity.

I saw that he wore the uniform of the dragoons, which was of cream trousers, red coat with gold frogging, and black boots. He was immaculately turned-out, and the whole effect overwhelmed me. I was used to seeing students in their fustian black; some poor scholars were almost threadbare, such matters had not been of consequence in Oxford, where learning was the criterion, not display. But now I glimpsed that this turn-out was essential to soldiery, where equipment, and persons, must always be on the alert.

"This way please, Miss," said Mrs Bagehot, a trifle coolly I thought. I knew that Philip Hellier stood at the foot of the stairs and watched us as we mounted the treads.

I found my room was larger than I expected, with a view of the lawns and trees of the front-garden. "When you have removed your cloak and unpacked," Mrs Bagehot said, "I will take you to Lady Deborah, for she is anxious to meet you."

Mrs Bagehot withdrew, and I freshened

myself to meet my new employer. I did not know that I was to face a woman of such beauty, presence and personality.

She lay in a huge fourposter bed, in a spacious room which also overlooked the front-lawns. Her face was pale, her large eyes shadowed with fatigue. Her dark brown hair lay upon the pillow and surrounded her face. Her glance was shrewd but welcoming. Her smile lit up her face with a rare quality of warmth and charm.

When the formalities were over, she bade me stand before her. "How slim and light you are, child! You are my build almost exactly. We can move swiftly and silently, you and I!

"Your eyes are good, hazel, with a touch of green. Your hair is brown like ash-bark, your skin very clear and without colour," she catalogued. "But we will soon put some glow into your cheeks with our Kent air!

"But who has dressed your hair for you, it is all drawn back as if in a snood! May I suggest that you wear it more loosely? There, come and read to me. I am working my way through the works of Molière, but I find the going hard! Perhaps we shall make progress when we tackle the volumes together. See! Here at the top of the page in the second act of La Malade Imaginaire. Let us each take parts, to make the reading more interesting. I will listen to your accent, and see if it matches mine."

Soon we were working away, reading the parts in the play, pausing to consider the nuances of a word or a phrase. I was astonished when a maid entered with a tray of tea.

I found that I was expected to have my meals with Lady Deborah, on a side table which the maid prepared. This arrangement pleased me, for I was dreading to meet the men of the household, particularly Philip. For I could not understand the emotions he had aroused in me.

Yet more than emotions, my heart thudded at the memory of him, my pulse raced, my breathing was disturbed. When I saw from the window of my room two men ride away from the house, I was relieved. I felt I needed to regain my equilibrium before I saw the General's nephew again.

* * *

That night, I had wild dreams. I seemed to be back in Oxford. I saw my father, Aunt Betsey and Gérard.

I heard the students' farewell cries, felt the pressure of their hands. I saw Gérard's red hair gleaming in the Oxford sunlight; heard the accented cadence of his voice.

I saw him in the moonlight climbing up the walls of the Great Hall; saw his darkly clothed figure moving along the guttering of its roof. For Gérard was an escaper. Nothing could hold him; nothing. He climbed the steepest slopes with ease; he feared no heights; locked rooms did not dismay him.

He told no one his secrets; but sometimes, for devilment, he would make his escape from bonds and enclosed rooms. Then suddenly, the image of him in my dreams began to fade. I awoke to find myself in my new bed, in my unaccustomed room at Charlecote Manor.

I arose to seek a drink of water. On my way back to bed I paused for a moment, and lifted the blind of the window. I saw a figure, insubstantial as a shade, flit across the lawn and into the shadow of a giant elm. There was no sound. No movement. My waking thoughts seemed as unsubstantial as my dream.

I settled into my new life and my new duties quickly. My tasks were not onerous, and Lady Deborah was appreciative and perceptive. Soon after my arrival I was called into the study to meet Sir Edmund.

I saw a man of around forty-five years of age; of medium height, with thick and well-dressed chestnut hair. I noticed that he wore no wig; I was to learn later that this mode of undressed hair had been introduced to the senior officers of the British Army by the Duke of Wellington.

The General's eyes were brown; his skin clear and fresh. He had a moustache, which did not hide his well-shaped mouth. His voice when he spoke was formal but kindly. I thought he had put aside his military bearing for the time being.

He bade me be seated, and said; "I remember your father as clearly as yesterday. We spent many happy hours together in Oxford. It is my privilege to honour the agreement of mutual assistance we made at our graduation. I feel honoured to welcome you to my house."

I murmured some reply, and the General resumed, "My wife, Lady Deborah, is of great concern to me. It is my wish that her days and hours are made as happy and pleasant as may be. I feel sure I may rely upon you to aid her in all ways possible. If you will do this, you will earn my gratitude and respect."

I felt touched by the very humane tone of the General's words and attitude. "I will do all possible," I said, "to earn the respect and regard of you both."

He seemed satisfied with my reply and with the interview. He bowed his head, and I withdrew.

The time sped swiftly by. I soon became accustomed to the ways of the household. I had my own leisure hours when I could walk in the garden; or take the carriage into Lyddford for shopping. When Lady Deborah was indisposed and the doctor called, we did no reading; but I sat by her bed to be within call.

I found that I got on well with the household staff, and particularly Mrs Bagehot, whose austere exterior hid a just and even disposition. I had some sympathy with her, for she appeared to have troubles of her own.

I saw her in conversation one afternoon in the hall with a young woman who was clearly in the early stages of pregnancy. Their raised voices carried to me.

"I will not accept their charity or his regrets. There is nothing he can do to make restitution. Will Shepherd has offered to marry me, and I have accepted his offer. To me, the matter is closed."

I heard Mrs Bagehot reply, "To marry except for affection is a serious step. And to hold such strong reservations in your heart is asking for trouble in the future."

"My actions are my own responsibility," the young woman replied. "You must grant me that. I take this step, to marry Will Shepherd, not to save anyone's face, but from my own inclination. You must leave me to solve my other commitment, in time."

The two women became aware then, that I was descending the stairs; they opened the green-baize door, and moved away. Later, Mrs Bagehot said, "That was my niece Belinda, who was until a short time ago, a housemaid in this house."

I soon became used to the coming and goings of military personnel connected with the Regiment. The General and Philip Hellier were officially stationed at the barracks in Lyddford, but they returned home as often as possible. I was soon to learn that the General valued his hours within Charlecote as the most precious of his life. His leisure hours seemed to give him the power to resume his important command.

For that his command was important, it was clear to see. We were near to the coast; beacons stood always at the ready. It was generally supposed that the Corsican would attack around Dover.

That the troops under the General were of prime importance to our country was obvious. I heard that the Prince of Wales himself had reviewed the General's troops, only recently.

But something of more significance to me than Napoleon, Prinny, and the invasion had occurred within the depths of my shy and inexperienced heart. I had fallen deeply, and wildly in love.

★ ★ ★

The emotions which I had experienced on first seeing Philip Hellier had been repeated, and intensified, when we again met.

The General asked me to take coffee with himself and Philip one evening after their supper, and the proximity of the young lieutenant had thrown me into disarray.

As Philip Hellier handed me my coffee cup, his hand brushed mine. The contact of his palm affected me deeply; it was as if my skin burned lightly; I know I blushed and buried my face in my coffee cup.

28

When he caught my eye he smiled slightly, with pleasure; as if this was an exercise that pleased him, and to see my discomfiture had added to his delight in the game.

The General noticed nothing and continued to talk to us. I knew his remarks were for my benefit to help me become familiar with the political situation and the tenor of events which ruled the house.

"The victories of Ulm, Austerlitz and Jena made the people of this country think that Napoleon is invincible.

"But he has Wellington to reckon with. The Duke has landed British troops in Portugal. Rebellion has also broken out in Spain.

"If only we can instil into our British soldiery the notion that the Emperor is fallible. That the British forces are more than a match for him. And this I believe with all my heart. I believe that Napoleon is a man, not a God, and can be defeated."

"The civilian population do not assist the soldiery, Uncle," Philip said. "Their dread of Napoleon is extreme. Plans are in hand for the civilian population to flee the coast in the event of invasion. I dread to think of the congestion on the roads, the panic, the hindrance to our troops."

"Yourself and Lady Deborah must hide in the cellars at the first hint of trouble," the General told me. "Be prepared at all times, Caroline," he added. "Keep a small case packed, and be ready to assist my wife."

The General soon bowed his head, and I left the room. Philip did not attempt to see me again that evening.

But shortly after this, one afternoon, we met in a bend of the stairs. To my surprise his arm shot out and around my waist, and he drew me to him.

It was in no way a close or amorous embrace; he held me lightly and his lips gently brushed my face.

No words were said; but my heart pounded, I flushed, my blood raced, and again I had the ridiculous sensation of burning on my skin where his lips had touched. I turned, and swiftly went on my way.

It was not until late one evening, when I was walking in the garden alone, at the termination of my duties with Lady Deborah, that he approached me with any expression of feeling. As I stepped into the shade of the giant elm which grew at one side of the lawn Philip himself stepped from its shadow, as if he had awaited me.

He clasped me suddenly in his arms and held me tightly. I felt the strength of his body; the power of his embrace. His lips found mine and pressed themselves upon me in a deep, close kiss. When he let me go, I fell from him, panting.

My emotions were now in a whirl; he had awakened within me impulses, inclinations which I had not known were part of my nature. The strength of my new sensations surprised me. I was dismayed to find another self within the one I thought I knew so well.

"How delicious it is to have your friendship, Caroline," Philip said. He spoke softly, as if not wishing to be overheard. "To have so delightful a female friend within the house! What more could a man ask?" he continued lightly. "But we must be circumspect, my dear. We must keep our friendship a secret. I would not wish my uncle and aunt to know of our closeness. Do you understand, poppet? It must be our secret, and ours alone."

I assented instantly. I would have agreed to any strategem to please him. He seemed satisfied. "Now continue your walk in the garden, alone. And I will go on my way to the barracks. Be sure not to reveal to prying ears that our friendship is deep and personal. There are watching eyes here, and I do not trust them."

I knew he referred to Mrs Bagehot, though why she should regard Philip with disapproval I did not know.

From this time on, our relationship grew apace. Nothing of moment took place, it is true, save the holding of hands, the stolen kisses, the secret meetings. But our love affair coloured my life with brilliance, and changed my whole perspective.

"Are you happy here, Caroline?" Lady Deborah asked me one day. "You seem to be so gay, so unlike the serious Miss who arrived a few months ago.

"Your skin has bloomed, you have

colour in your cheeks and brightness in your eyes. It must be our channel breezes which have transformed you! Bring me the Latin primer, dear, and we will resume our studies."

I did not know what the malady could be from which Lady Deborah was suffering. But there were many wasting and debilitating diseases without names, at this time.

She spent her days mostly in bed; though sometimes she got up a little in her room. The General spent some time with her each time he visited Charlecote, and his care and concern for her were wonderful to see.

One day, I was standing by the window of Lady Deborah's room, adjusting a blind, when I saw a young lady enter the garden from a carriage which had drawn up at the gate.

I saw that she was of medium height, very slender, and about her there was an air of great style.

Her fair hair was beautifully arranged in a coil with tendrils around the face. Her dress I saw was very stylish, made in a long straight panel from beneath the bosom, and falling without hindrance to her feet.

She carried a parasol, for it was August and the weather was warm. She walked with a sure but gentle pace towards the front door.

"Who have you seen? What has captured your attention?" Lady Deborah asked me.

When I described the new visitor to Charlecote, Lady Deborah said, "That will be Lydia Clements. How accurate your description is, my dear! Yes, she is both beautiful and stylish, and as pleasant in her disposition as she is in her outward aspect.

"She has been for several months in Bath, but Edmund had told me she had now returned. Her parents are sometime friends of the family, and Lydia comes and goes as she pleases, and is always welcome here."

I looked again from the window, just in time to see Miss Clements pass underneath the shade of the giant elm.

For a few moments her figure was hidden, shrouded in the shadowed gloom. Then she emerged into the sunshine and left the darkness of the tree behind her.

But in some amazing and incredible way, it was as if the shadow of the tree remained upon her person.

She moved forward, still veiled in shadow; then she vanished beneath the portico of the front of the house; and we heard the bell ring, distantly, below.

3

IT was true, Lydia Clements was as affable as she was attractive, and without being overt or forward she made it clear to me that my friendship would be welcome to her, and that she valued my approval.

But I felt grave self-doubts about myself in relation to this young lady. For I felt home-spun beside her, gauche, and of little account.

When she had gone, Lady Deborah bade me approach her bed. "Dear Caroline, I have been thinking," she said. "I have two new gowns expected from Madame Serle in Lyddford, and I feel I shall never have the opportunity to wear them.

"You and I are the same size. Madame Serle is due to call today. If you will accept these gowns from me, and regard them as a gift . . . It would please me more than I could say.

"Also, Madame Serle brings her assistant

with her, to dress my hair. I will request that she will also dress yours, if you will wish this.

"Thus . . . " Lady Deborah's words trailed away. But it was clear to me that she wished me to meet Miss Lydia Clements on equal ground; that she did not wish Lydia to eclipse me, or to cause me embarrassment or distress.

When the dressmaker came she brought with her her pattern dolls; and Lady Deborah instantly became engaged in choosing three new outfits for some problematical future date. Madam Serle tried the two finished dresses on me, and did what alterations were necessary on the spot.

I was more than glad to say farewell to my old-fashioned dresses with wide skirts and flounces. I loved the new Empire style; I liked also my new hairstyle which coiled in tendrils about my face. Lady Deborah's pleasure matched mine, and when the General entered the room at around six o'clock, we were both in a happy mood and pleased with events. The effect upon Philip was dramatic.

"What have you done to yourself?" he

37

asked me, as he drew me swiftly into the study. We were safe for a few moments, while the General was upstairs. "I always thought you would develop into a lovely woman, but you are a beauty already. Oh Caroline, my dear!" And Philip crushed me in his arms, and prevented me from speaking with his kiss.

Happiness flooded through me. I had found the man I loved, I told myself, and he in turn loved me. How quickly my life had developed; how speedily had events opened up before me! For that we should eventually be married, Philip and I, I was now sure. My way in life seemed set; there seemed to be only happiness and fulfilment ahead.

I was surprised that Philip had not mentioned our future engagement before this. That evening, after dinner, when we met secretly in the tiny arbour set to one side of the lawn, I said to him:

"May I not tell Lady Deborah of our love? I long to share our secret with her. She has been so kind to me. She shows so much interest in my life, I long to share my happiness with her. I feel sure she would approve and wish us well."

Philip's reaction astonished me. He seized my arm suddenly, and held it tightly. "No, Caroline. Certainly not. No one must know of our attachment. At least, not at this moment, my dear.

"Truth to tell I am in the midst of difficulties, and this is not the moment for me to take on further responsibilities.

"I am the recipient of the proceeds of a trust fund, set up by my family. But unfortunately, both interest and capital have come into the hands of userers.

"I feel I can recoup the position, if I am given time. In addition, I do not wish my uncle to know of my monetary difficulties. I feel sure these facts would be revealed if I announced any engagement.

"Therefore Caroline . . . Let our affection be our secret only, at the present time. This is my definite wish. I ask you, if you care for me, to honour this."

Of course I promised. I would have done anything to aid him. I wished I had money to succour him; I told him that I would help him in any way that I could.

He held me in his arms and kissed me gently. It was as if his circumstances were a brake upon the demands of his love.

I had now become aware of other conditions which were part of the life at Charlecote Manor. Not only were military personnel frequent visitors; but there were other, insubstantial, more shadowy personages moving on mysterious occasions after darkness, or in the small hours of the morning.

My window overlooked the side-lawns also, and a rounded gate, set well-back in the high wall and shrouded with ivy and shrubs. On several occasions I saw vague shapes move through this gate, and towards the french windows of the General's study. I heard distant voices, but caught no words.

I did not mention these circumstances to anyone, for it was no affair of mine. And indeed, I had now entered upon what was for me the happiest time, so far, of my life.

Lydia sought me out in gay and friendly fashion, and often included me in her plans. Philip, who had known Lydia for many years, was often drawn in to escort us; and the three of us made several excursions to the coast; and once we attended a reception at Lyddford Barracks.

Lydia was gay and artless in her enjoyment of these outings. Indeed, there was a shade of naiveté beneath her outwardly sophisticated appearance. She was also a gifted artist, and would sit for hours with her sketching block and pencils before a scene or object which had attracted her attention.

Perhaps it was this artistic trait in her, I told myself, that made her a little ingenuous. But her gaiety was infectious; she was the first woman friend I had ever had, and my enjoyment was tinged with gratitude to her. She treated me always as an equal, as if I matched herself in looks and poise.

"Lydia and her family put a good face upon things," Lady Deborah said to me one day. "They are quite impoverished, over at Copthwaite Hall, yet you would never think this to see and meet Lydia.

"Her wardrobe is quite small, yet she makes a satisfactory appearance by switching her garments around. Have you noticed, Caroline? And her artistic taste enables her to present herself in a charming way.

"I hear her parents are quite pressed for money," Lady Deborah continued, yet she spoke entirely without rancour or malice. For like all invalids Lady Deborah loved an innocent gossip; and her comments were kindly observations only, and were accepted as such.

"But Lydia has expectations, I believe," Lady Deborah concluded at last. "But from where, I do not know. And when, it would be impossible to say."

Lady Deborah willingly gave me leave to attend these new entertainments with Philip and Lydia. At first she shared in my pleasure; then suddenly, a note of warning appeared in her voice.

"For a woman to find the man she can love for a lifetime, is truly her destiny, and the most important event in her existence.

"But before that, Caroline . . . Men may deceive. Many men enjoy their little adventures, their pleasing conquests. It is an art and a necessary quality of life to know when a man is serious, and when he is playing a game. Take care, Caroline. Your nature, sheltered in Oxford, is trusting and vulnerable. I could not bear to see you hurt, or betrayed."

But I took no countenance of her words. Indeed, I considered them generalities, which did not apply to me! Yet their wisdom must have penetrated to my mind. For one day, on the promenade at Deal, while Lydia was sketching a fishing boat on the beach, I blurted out a question to Philip concerning our marriage.

"Marriage!" the word was uttered by Philip with more than surprise. There was almost outrage in his tone. "Take care not to reveal our position before Lydia!" He drew me further along the promenade — "But of course, my dear," he said placatingly, "we will be married in time. My financial position is improving. I have hopes to be in better straits, before long. But in the meantime . . . Let us continue as we are. We are blessed to see each other frequently. And Lydia's outings are a good cover for our meetings, in the future."

43

It was at this moment that we saw, walking along the promenade together, the figure of a young pregnant woman, accompanied by a man.

The man was tall and broadly built; clearly an artisan of some consequence. "This is Will Shepherd, the landlord of The Three Plumes Inn in Lyddford." Philip did not add any comment as to the identity of the young woman. But I recognised her at once as Belinda Bagehot.

Felicitations were exchanged; though these were cool on Belinda's part. "May I wish you every happiness upon your betrothal," Philip said. I thought for once his charm and ease of manner had deserted him. Will Shepherd flushed, I saw his fists clench and unclench — He answered no words. After a moment's awkward silence, the couple passed on their way.

For some reason this encounter disturbed me. Lydia also seemed perturbed. "I would not have thought it possible of Will Shepherd, to cause such distress to Belinda and Mrs Bagehot," she said. "And Belinda too, must bear some blame for her condition."

Somehow, our outing was spoiled. "It is later than I thought," Philip said. "Let us go back to the carriage, for I must report to the barracks within an hour."

He had gone deathly pale, and I thought he knew more about the affairs of Belinda and Will Shepherd than he wished to disclose. Perhaps a trooper in his regiment had transgressed, and in this way he bore some responsibility for the situation — No further comment was made, and we returned to Charlecote without delay.

That evening, I had occasion to go to the General's study on an errand for Lady Deborah. I entered the oak-panelled, book-lined room with trepidation, and interest. For this was forbidden territory to all staff; a military trooper cleaned and tidied this room.

I saw there were maps upon a stand, a globe stood on its plinth, the European stations outlined in red with tiny coloured flags indicating areas of special importance. Lady Deborah had embroidered a book-cover for her husband, and it was this she wished me to lay on his desk, as a surprise. I hesitated by the desk, fearing to intrude into a sphere in which I guessed I would not be welcome.

It was at this moment that I heard the sound of a movement at the french window. One of the doors of the window opened, and from the darkness outside, a figure stepped into the room.

I stared at this man with surprise. He was tall and thin, and wore the stained and blackened garments of a glazier. Indeed, he carried the leather-bag of his trade slung from one shoulder. His face was partly obscured by the cowl of his habit, but I saw that his hands and cheeks were streaked with the grime and dust of his occupation.

He spoke no word, and appeared to look at me with equal surprise — When I had recovered my wits, I deemed it my duty to speak to him. "I think you have made a mistake," I said. "If you seek Mrs Bagehot, the housekeeper, about some matter concerning the household, the tradesmen's entrance is at the rear of the house."

"Thank you, Miss," he answered. His

words were muffled. "I appreciate the information. But I seek to speak with General Sir Edmund Franklyn. I was told I would find him here."

"You are fortunate to have made your way so far," I answered. "Troopers are on watch around these grounds — I wonder you have not been apprehended."

I saw a flash of amusement in his eyes. "In my employment we learn to move without attracting attention," he replied sardonically. "I trust you will not summon assistance and turn me over to the military."

There was almost a teasing quality in his tone as he spoke, which I could not place. "You are certainly in the wrong to enter the General's study," I said firmly. "I certainly cannot leave you here, alone, while I summon assistance."

"Then we must be companions in solitude," he replied. "Keeping guard upon one another. I personally could not have wished for a more comely and courageous jailer."

I flushed at his words; I could not understand this man, I felt bewildered by his presence and proximity. At this moment we were spared any more discourse as the door of the room opened, and the General came in.

He was astounded, not to see the glazier, but to see myself. I hastened to explain my presence, and held towards him the embroidered cover which I had been holding. That Lady Deborah had transgressed in sending me upon this errand, and not myself for executing it, was plain. But the General recovered himself instantly. "Please leave the study now, Caroline," he said. "I will ask to see you later. Also my wife. And do not mention this incident to anyone, please."

Alone in my room, I pondered the strange incident — The figure of the glazier seemed to haunt me. His appearance and mode of address intrigued me. I felt suddenly that I would like to observe him more closely, to try to make some evaluation of him in my mind. I drew on my cloak and went downstairs. I stepped into the garden.

That the glazier had come into the garden through the hidden gate, I was sure — I therefore stationed myself beneath the giant elm, so that I could see the moment of his departure.

I watched the lighted square of the study window, over which the curtains were now drawn. When the lights went out, and the curtains were drawn aside, I was alerted — Sure enough, the door of the french window opened, and the shadowy figure stepped outside.

Scarcely seeming to disturb the gloom, the glazier passed over the lawn — But on the verge of the shadows of the giant elm he stopped; his senses on guard. I peered from the shadows, and I knew he had seen me.

He laughed softly, and also stepped into the shade of the tree — Then before I could protest or move away he caught me in his arms, bent back my head, and kissed me full upon the lips.

Surprise, more than outrage or anger, welled within me. I was pressed into his blackened habit; I could smell the putty, the steel of his tools, the dust of the panes of glass, the male aroma of a man engaged in his trade. I felt also arms like iron bands, and a body lean and hard as steel itself. And lips that were hard also; yet poised to take and receive the sweetness of a kiss's sensation.

When he released me I fell back against the trunk of the huge elm. He said no word, but gave a short soft cry of laughter. I saw his head go back as he laughed; his eyes still observing me. In the dark light I saw then that his eyes were clear grey, almost translucent, clear and transparent as water. Then the cowl of his habit fell across his face, and he was gone.

I heard the gate close softly, and distantly the faint cry of a trooper. I realised also that the light had come on in the General's study, and that the french window had opened again.

I saw the General emerge, very stiff and upright; he crossed the lawn and stood before me as I sheltered still beneath the lowering elm.

"Caroline," he said. "Will you please enter the study. I wish to speak with you. And upon a matter of importance. Come this way, please."

And the General gestured to me to precede him. Very shaken, greatly wondering, and not a little afraid, I bowed my head to accede to the General's request — And so I crossed the lawn, and entered the lighted study. The General followed, drew the curtains across the window, went to the door, and turned the key in the lock. He faced me and said, "Sit down."

I sat in a chair before the desk and faced the General. I awaited his opening words.

4

"SO you have met the glazier."

The words were a statement and not a question, and I did not reply, for I thought no reply was called for. The General did not seat himself at his desk, but paced about the big room, his head sunk upon his chest, clearly in deep thought.

He glanced at me once, and it was a measuring glance; as if he was judging my worth, and whether to speak to me frankly or dismiss me with some facile excuse or explanation. When he spoke, it was clear that he had made up his mind.

He seated himself at his desk. "In any warfare, there are other factors which are essential to victory, apart from the bearing of arms in the field," he said.

"Information is perhaps the most important aid to victory a commander-in-chief can have. Information, up-to-date, accurate, and correctly interpreted.

Without these, no battles can be fought and no wars won."

The General paused, and I heard the silence of the house around us. "This regiment, the 18th Dragoons, is not only commissioned to guard the most vulnerable stretch of coast which faces Napoleon, but is equipped and trained to leave these shores at the behest of the Duke of Wellington at any time.

"Reserves would take our places," he told me. "But until we receive our orders we are stationed here and our movements are governed by the direct command of the Duke, who himself entrusted me with this commission and issued personal instructions."

And now the General paused, and it was clear that he was approaching the nub and purpose of his discourse. I steeled myself as if an ordeal was approaching. For I guessed that the General's words and intelligence would be of some moment, and I would need all my wits about me fully to comprehend his words and his inner meanings.

"You will know that the European battle-front against the Emperor Bonaparte is fully stretched. Austria, Prussia," he said. "Spain, Portugal, Italy are all embroiled, as well as France itself.

"The Duke of Wellington wishes to receive vital and up to the minute information on military and political matters from all these countries.

"He has therefore personally instructed a corps of hand-picked men to serve him and their country in this particular way.

"These men travel in the country of their designation, often in disguise, often in great danger, mixing with military personnel, and, in their own way, seeking out the information their commander-in-chief requires."

"They are spies," I ventured to say.

"The Duke prefers to designate them as personal aides. The word agent is the one he prefers.

"Secrecy is of the utmost importance," the General resumed. "The agents clearly cannot report their activities openly, in a military barracks. So it was decided that Charlecote itself should be the place to which they should report, and from where they should receive their further instructions."

I remembered now not only the shadowy figures who came to the study at Charlecote at night, but also the frequent attendance of military personnel around Charlecote. It was clear that despatch-riders would be required, secretaries, translators, emissaries from the Duke. A vital part of the war effort was located in this house. Behind the high walls of Charlecote an essential part of the war was being waged.

"The glazier whom you saw was one of my most trusted agents, recently returned from Spain. He had information of high importance to transmit. He has returned to his post, without furlough or leave. I value his life highly, and trust he will return."

I remembered suddenly the tall figure of the glazier, his lean face caught in a shaft of light through the leaves of the elm tree, his eyes clear as water, with a penetrating but mocking regard.

"Sir, am I to believe that you are the head of the secret service serving the Duke of Wellington?" I asked.

An expression of relief passed over the General's face. It was as if he had arrived at the point where he must inform me of his own position in the organisation, and had hesitated to proclaim himself its head.

I marvelled at the sensitivity and humility of this remarkable man, who could serve with distinction so eminent and hard a taskmaster as the Iron Duke. He was a man of many shades, I thought — Husband to Lady Deborah, uncle to Philip Hellier; kindly master to the servants of his household. That he held so powerful a Regiment as the 18th Dragoons in a sure command was something he would not deem remarkable; but to myself, an onlooker, it appeared exceptional. And now, to learn that he was in addition the head of the Duke's secret network of agents . . . I was stunned by the revelation of the many-sided character of this man.

"I have disclosed to you this information, not because there was placed upon me any necessity to reveal to you the truth." The General paused. "Indeed, I could have dismissed yourself and the matter with an explanation of mistaken identity which might have satisfied your curiosity and interest. But instead, I decided to entrust you with the truth. I trust that you will appreciate what I have done, and in the future return my trust with your compliance with my wishes."

Something in the General's tone prompted me to rise to my feet. I stood before the desk, and faced the General, who had also risen.

"Secrecy. The strictest secrecy is required. Nothing more is asked of you, Caroline, save that you should regard the matter upon which I have spoken to you as one requiring silence and discretion — Believe me, upon silence and discretion so much depends."

"I am honoured by your confidence, sir," I answered. "Please believe I can keep a still tongue when required, and that I shall honour your trust by my silence and discretion."

I could not add that I would forget the whole matter, for nothing could erase from my mind the memory of the glazier, and the General's words. Indeed, I felt a flush stain my cheeks as I remembered the glazier's kiss. The General looked at me keenly, then bowed his head, and escorted me to the door. There he paused, and said:

"Napoleon Bonaparte is poised over Europe like a falcon who wishes to hold the entire western world in his grasp.

"He has conquered so much already. And believe me, he is planning to invade Russia! But Britain must be his last and final prize. It is Britain he is waiting to grasp in his claws, to conquer, and to tear apart.

"I shall rely upon your assurance of silence," the General finished. "I accept your word as if upon oath."

I returned the General's level gaze; I saw his deep brown eyes, his thick chestnut hair, the dignity and grace of his carriage in his military uniform. He took my hand for a moment in a formal salute, smiled at me in kindly fashion and continued to talk for a moment — Then the door of the study closed behind me, and the interview was done.

★ ★ ★

Upstairs, alone in my room, I had much to consider. That the General had honoured me by entrusting me with information concerning the network of agents and his part in the organisation, was plain.

I thought of the glazier. I remembered the sudden sweetness of his kiss; the shaft of happiness which had flooded through me.

I chided myself. How could I possibly feel these sensations when I was already given, at least by word, to another man? For, in spite of the secrecy which Philip had imposed upon me I regarded myself as unofficially engaged to him, and I considered myself as standing in relationship to him of his future wife.

I drew aside the curtain of my window, and looked out at the darkling scene. The branches and foliage of the giant elm towered in solitary grandeur at the edge of the lawn; the gate was still. But I knew that sentries patrolled, without.

I remembered the General's final words, as he paused before he opened the study door. "To speak on another plane, I want you to know how much I appreciate your efforts for the comfort and wellbeing of my wife.

"Her health has improved enormously since you arrived to be her companion. And with her health, her spirits have risen, and she takes a more hopeful attitude towards her life in general.

"She says you read excellently, with feeling and interest. And your conversation with her in the French tongue, and your assistance with her compositions have given her a sense of achievement — Please know your efforts have not gone unremarked, and I value your services in my household."

The next day was a busy one for me, for Lady Deborah took it into her head to get up, and she walked for sometime around her room. She then became fatigued, and had to be helped back into bed. So that I was glad when Lydia called, for her chatter and kindliness were a distraction to the invalid. She had with her her sketching pad, and she sat beside Lady Deborah's bed.

"Look, I will show you my latest sketches," Lydia said. "When you are better, will you sit for me? I would love to draw your head and shoulders. See, here is a sketch of the promenade at

Deal." She turned towards me. "I made the preliminary sketches that day you, Philip and I went — Do you remember, Caroline? Look, there is a ketch, and a vessel further out at sea. I have tried to catch the texture of the sand. And the clouds. They are difficult, but not impossible . . . "

Her voice rippled on, her enthusiasm and gaiety capturing our attention. She went through her sketch-book, showing us her drawings one by one. It was not until the final sketch, that a strange incident occurred.

On her sketching-block I saw a drawing of a roughly made hut; an affair of twigs and branches and interlaced boughs. It stood in a clearing in a wood or forest; trees deeply surrounded it; the ground was rough, as if a clearing had been made for the hut from the surrounding thorns and undergrowth.

"Where is this, Lydia?" Lady Deborah asked.

Lydia laughed. "It is the woodcutter's hut in Gartham Woods," she said. "I go there sometimes when I wish to be alone to work out my ideas. It is very quiet there. Very silent." She spoke no further word, and we continued to look at her drawings.

Then as she moved, the shadow of her head slid away from the paper. But not for me. For as before, when Lydia had stepped out from under the elm tree and the shadow had remained upon her person, so now, to my eyes, a shadow remained over the sketch of the woodcutter's hut.

But instantly, the illusion was obscured as Winifrede brought in tea, and the sketch-book was laid aside. And soon there was only the sound of our happy voices in the room, the rattle of teacups and our laughter. And all doubts were stilled in the pleasure of the congenial company; in the warmth and reassurance of the agreeable and friendly occasion.

5

TIME passed swiftly, then suddenly, quite out of the blue Lady Deborah decided to give a dinner-party. "And I shall come down for it," she said. "You noticed how well I did the other day, when I was walking about the bedroom. With Edmund to assist me, I am sure I can reach the drawing-room. Then I have only to sit down to receive my guests, and later, walk to the dining-room. Yes. That is it. That is what we will do. Caroline, I need your help."

I was all attention instantly, for the doctor had told me that any activity within the circle of the home that could catch Lady Deborah's attention, would be beneficial to her. "Please send a message to Madame Serle to call again, and bring her dolls. I shall need a new gown. And you also, Caroline. Do not deny it! Do not flout me! You must have a dinner-gown, a trifle decoletté, you have nothing like that in your wardrobe, have you? And make a date for her assistant to coiffeur our hair. She dressed your hair so becomingly before, Caroline, I look forward to seeing what she can do a second time. Now as for kid pumps . . . "

Lady Deborah's voice rattled on, she was suddenly gay and outgoing. When I had sent the message to Madame Serle she said, "Caroline, please take the carriage and go down to the Three Plumes Inn, in Lyddford, and speak to the landlord, Will Shepherd on my behalf.

"Tell him that I would like to hire two of his best serving-waiters for the night of the dinner-party. We shall also require additional wines. Burgundy, dry sack, cognac, foreign liquers. And ask him also if he can procure a side of venison. The men will love this, Caroline! Mrs Bagehot will simmer it in herbs and gravy, and for the ladies we will have guinea-fowl baked on a bed of soft fruits.

"The serving-waiters will assist Mrs Bagehot and Winifrede to serve the viands. What a pity that Belinda . . . "

Lady Deborah stopped, instantly regretting her words. I saw a shadow pass across her face, but she recovered instantly. "And give to Will Shepherd my personal greetings. If he could spare the time to visit me concerning the dinner-party, I would appreciate this very much."

I took the carriage, as I was bid, and was driven to the Three Plumes. The inn was closed, but upon hearing the coachman's voice, the bolts were drawn and the inn door opened. A burly figure in shirt-sleeves and leather apron bade me enter. Will Shepherd then took off his apron, and put on his coat.

I saw that the landlord was a man of powerful physique, but quiet manners. I guessed that he would have no trouble with unruly troopers in this garrison town; but that his manner of dealing with them would be smooth and harmless. He had thick auburn hair (almost to Gérard's redness) and steady blue eyes. His cheeks were ruddy, his hands well-formed, well-cared for and capable.

"Please to tell her ladyship that I will do all she asks for her dinner-party," the landlord of the inn told me. "And

I will call to see her personally, without delay.

"She will know without doubt, of the marriage of Belinda and myself almost a year ago, and that three months later Belinda was safely delivered of a fine baby boy.

"We call him George," he said. "After his Majesty the king. George Shepherd," he added firmly, so that there could be no mistake over that.

I thanked the innkeeper whom I liked instinctively, and turned to go. Then a door of the inn which led to the house at the rear opened, and Belinda came in. She stood and watched me silently, but uttered no word.

I saw that she was slim now, and pleasantly rounded. There was a quiet dignity about her, which matched her husband's mien. Her brown hair was drawn back; her well-shaped mouth was still, not smiling. I begged to take my leave of them both; again I felt a sense of dismay as I turned to go. But I chided myself inwardly, for surely their marriage and affairs were no possible concern of mine.

Back at Charlecote, there was a flurry of activity. The General had been to see Lady Deborah, and requested that he might speak with me in the study. I took my cloak off hastily, and went with all speed to this private room.

The General was seated at his desk, with papers before him. "Caroline," he said, "I seek your help, and I trust you will give it. For Sergeant Summerson, who is my chief interpreter, has met with an accident, and cannot give me his services to translate this latest despatch.

"The despatch is in Spanish," he said. "And I understand from my wife that you are conversant with this language. Therefore, if you could peruse this document, and tell me its contents, it will oblige me and save me much effort and inconvenience. Take your own time. Sit in this chair, before the desk. Let me see what you can do."

I sat down as I was bade and took the sheaf of papers from the General. Yes, the intelligence was written in Spanish, much of it in Spanish script, some of it colloquial in barrack-room language. There were personal letters also, and pages from a diary, with rough notes. Clearly these papers had been taken from the study or case of a highly-placed military man. I agreed with the General's estimation that they were important.

I suddenly found that I was delighted to be using my knowledge of the Iberian tongue once again. French I used often with Lady Deborah; but there had been no call at all for Spanish in my life at Charlecote. I read all the papers through once, then made a verbal report upon the general gist of the documents. "But I would like more time," I said. "I would like to make a full and accurate translation, and put the manuscript before you."

"So you shall," said the General. "That is just what I wish. I shall be absent from the study at the barracks for the next few hours. Work at this corner desk, near to the window. You will be undisturbed here, and I will personally visit my wife and request your leave of absence from your duties upstairs."

The General went, and I began my work. My ideas were lame and halting at first, when I came to decipher the more abstruse parts of the documents; then suddenly, it was as if I was back in Oxford again; back amid the piles of books and students' essays; seeing the students' lamps as they studied and talked into the night; listening to the never-ending, time-recording peal of the college bells.

When I had finished I laid the manuscript upon the desk, and went upstairs. I did not know that a major step had been taken in my destiny, and in my life.

★ ★ ★

I did not know also, that in distant Hampshire an old lady living alone except for an aged servant, had been taken ill in the night. An event which would lead to other events which would have a dramatic effect upon all our lives.

★ ★ ★

And then a strange and unexpected incident occurred. Lady Deborah said to me, "An Inspector General is visiting the barracks shortly, and Edmund has organised a reception in his honour. Philip will be going, of course, and he has asked Lydia to accompany him."

I was pleased to hear of the reception, and the invitation. I wondered which dress I could wear, as of course, I thought, I shall be included in the invitation to the reception. Philip would escort both Lydia and myself, as he had done previously at the smaller affair at the barracks. No doubt he would tell me soon, or Lydia would mention it. But as the day wore on no word was said, though I encountered both Lydia and Philip. Later that evening, after dinner, I met Philip on the stairs.

"I am pleased to know of the reception at the barracks," I said. "What is the time of this? I must have warning, to make my preparations."

Philip looked at me curiously. "You have received an invitation to the reception?" he said.

"Why no," I answered. "I considered . . . " I was sure your own invitation would cover both Lydia and myself, I thought, though I could not bring myself to say the words.

70

"I am so sorry about this, Caroline," Philip said, "but the list of guests this time is limited. One officer, one guest. The adjutant has specified no . . . " I thought he was going to say 'hangers-on' but his tongue stayed at the word.

He turned from me. I could not believe that this was happening to me. That the man I loved, to whom I was committed for life, in my own mind, was rejecting me. "Philip," I said. I could not believe he was going to take Lydia to the reception, and not myself. "Philip". I could not bring myself to utter any words of reproach, or question his motives. Through a haze of tears I watched his back in its red jacket retreat from me upstairs.

Later that evening as I was going up to bed, Philip stepped out from a secondary landing, and caught me in his arms. I felt his powerful embrace, his strength, his nearness. He held my head captive against his shoulder, and kissed me ardently upon the lips.

"I am sorry not to be able to take you to the reception," he breathed. "Believe me, it is not my wish. Expediency alone dictates that I must take Lydia. But my heart is not in it. Believe me, my heart will be at home, here, with you. Wait for me, Caroline. Everything will come right, if you will only be patient, and wait."

Swiftly, he went to his own room. He was like a man who feared to be caught in a misdemeanour. I pondered his words, and tried to draw comfort from his kiss. But again my tears fell as I began to undress. I drew the curtain and looked at the giant elm. But the gate was closed, and there was no activity outside, this night.

★ ★ ★

The next morning the General sent for me, and congratulated me upon my translation of the Spanish despatch. "I have been considering this matter," he said, as I stood in front of the desk before him. "And I wonder if you will undertake further translations of Spanish despatches for me?

"The Sergeant translator has other duties, and is not always available. I feel that with you within the house, and sometimes free from your duties with my wife . . . It might be possible for you to assist me."

"I should be pleased to do this, if Lady Deborah agrees," I answered.

"My wife says she is sufficiently recovered to be seated, sometimes, in a chair before the window, and to observe the garden and the gardeners. She thus feels she will not require so much attention. If in this free time which is coming available to you, you could undertake this work for me . . . " The General stopped. "The organisation would be grateful to you, and you would assist the agents and their efforts at home and overseas."

There was a small ante-room nearby, which was little used. Under the General's orders, this was simply furnished with a chair and a desk, with lamps and a small room-heater. I understood that this was to be my own small sanctum, to which I could repair to work upon the Spanish translations. I was thrilled and delighted by this tiny space, which seemed to put a new seal upon my services at Charlecote Manor.

My position at Charlecote had been very acceptable before, it was true. I had been given every courtesy and assistance by the staff, in my efforts for Lady Deborah. I had come to like and esteem Mrs Bagehot; and I felt this regard, though austerely held in check, was returned. But now, a clear advancement in my status was taking place.

As soon as it was known that I was now also working for the General in some unspecified though clerical service; and had my own room in which to perform these duties, the staff of the household could not conceal their respect.

I became suddenly Miss Lancing to the staff, though I had not sought this appellation, and felt embarrassed by it. Offers of help to ease my new labours abounded; Winifrede offered to launder my hose; hot chocolate was instantly produced when I worked late with the despatches. I made light of these matters and my efforts to Lady Deborah; but she herself seemed impressed that the General had entrusted me with this work. But I was determined that she should not suffer, and did not spare myself to be with her as much as I possibly could.

The dinner-party had had to be postponed, as the General had been obliged to leave Charlecote and Lyddford on a mission which he did not specify. "It is difficult organising a party for military men," Lady Deborah said finally. "Firstly Edmund. And now I have heard that my brother will also be on duty. And I had dearly hoped that he would attend."

"Your brother?" I asked, rather startled. Then I remembered that Lady Deborah had mentioned her brother it seemed a long time ago, when she had told me of her parents and her early life.

"He is serving with the Royal Blues," she told me, rather proudly, I thought. "These are Prinny's own chosen troops, his bodyguard, and his close associates.

"They are stationed at Brighton, now. This confounds my brother a little, for he would prefer to serve overseas in the thick of the fighting. But the Prince of Wales has commanded otherwise. He wishes my brother to attend him, and this is, of course, an honour of the highest order.

Yet it is a tight commission, and my brother can seldom get away.

"They say that the Prince of Wales is back again with Mrs Fitzherbert," Lady Deborah went on. "Oh she is charming, in her plump and comfortable way. Some say they are married already! But I do not believe this. I think the marriage with Caroline of Brunswick was a legal one, and Mrs Fitzherbert is a usurper only. My brother could no doubt tell us much, but he never betrays the Prince's confidence, and never speaks of these things."

I only half listened to her words, for I had heard the talk of Prinny before, and speculation about his attachment. I did not know it, but distantly, in Hampshire, an old lady passed away. And so all our lives were immediately altered, and changed.

* * *

"Lydia has inherited money! Her Aunt, Lady Hawkins, who lives near Salisbury, has passed away and left Lydia her estate. Lydia is an heiress! She has become a rich woman, at last!"

I felt a shock of astonishment at these tidings. Coming from the family of an impoverished scholar, I was unused to having relations who could pass away, distantly, and leave an estate. When Lydia came to see us, she was overcome with joy.

"It is not that I do not mourn my Aunt Keziah," she said. "Though I do not remember her greatly. I have not seen her since childhood!

"Yet I cannot hide from anyone my joy that at last I can assist my parents at Copthwaite Hall. And also, for myself . . . " She held outwards a little the skirt of her dress, and I was surprised to see that this was a new model of fawn silk, with a belt of brocade high beneath the breast.

"The lawyer has brought me an advance of money," she told us, rather defensively. "And of course, I purchased new clothes! I shall have a new gown for the Inspector-General's reception. A new cloak. New pumps! And Madame Serle's assistant shall do my hair."

"Rejoice with me, Caroline," Lydia

cried. And she caught me in her arms and whirled me around, as if we were dancing to some remote and invisible music.

Lady Deborah laughed aloud with joy, watching us; but somehow, a shadow passed over my mind, and would not be dissipated.

The mention of the reception had hurt me; and though I rejoiced over Lydia's good fortune, I guessed that her new wealth might erect a barrier between us. I thought our innocent friendship, based on mutual appreciation, might not survive her beckoning new life.

On the night of the reception I worked in my tiny room, busy deciphering a Spanish despatch. Mrs Bagehot herself brought me sandwiches and camomile tea; I applied myself diligently to my translation, trying to keep the image of Philip and Lydia together, from my mind.

And now, in retrospect, I can see that from this time a change came over the relationship of Philip, Lydia and myself. Before this incident of the Inspector General's reception, we had been three equal friends. Enjoying one another's company, with no evasions or barriers.

Philip and I had hidden our love, it is true; but Lydia had an ingenuous nature, and this reticence on our part did not harm her. But now, Lydia and Philip became a duo; and I was the one who was left out.

I tried not to be hurt by the situation. I tried to believe in his love. He sought me out, when he could, and caught me in his arms and kissed me. I clung to him, wanting to believe that he loved me, wanting our old relationship to return.

I did not reproach him that I was omitted from his arrangements. My pride would not allow me to reprove him for his absences from my side. One evening he said, "I want to assure you of my love for you, Caroline. Please believe that. I love you totally, my dear. I ask you again to wait. We will be married, I promise you, in time.

"Circumstances hem me in, but I shall find a way through. Therefore, do not despair. I shall come to you before too long, and formally ask you to be my wife. And how I long for that day! Believe in me, Caroline. We shall be together, in the end."

This was the declaration for which I had yearned for some time, and his words healed some of the unhappiness in my heart. I did believe in him, I told myself, and I would wait as he requested me, and believe that everything would work out for us, in the fullness of time.

And then, like a forest fire a rumour ran around the house that an engagement was imminent. I heard the domestic staff whispering. I even heard Mrs Bagehot discussing the possibility with Winifrede. But who was getting engaged to whom, it was not stated. It could be Prinny and Mrs Fitzherbert! I told myself. And then, the mythical rumour died down.

But the impression remained in my mind that Philip had solved his difficulties. And that soon he would come to me and formally propose.

I pondered the implications of this move upon the household at Charlecote. Would the General and Lady Deborah welcome me as a member of their family? What would Aunt Betsey say, when she knew I was not to marry a scholar? Would Lydia grant us her blessing, and move out of our lives? No doubt Lydia had her own plans made by this time, I thought. Her money would give her mobility and advancement. No doubt she would marry a gentleman with a title, or other social advantages. For she loved social life and the fripperies of sophisticated concourse. And all these were open to her, since she had inherited her aunt's money.

And then difficulties of another nature solved themselves and the General returned to Britain's shores. "We can have the dinner-party now, Caroline," Lady Deborah told me. "The date is a fortnight from today. Let us go over the guest list again, and make our final preparations!"

And so we were plunged into a whirlwind of effort, preparing the house and the feast to come. We did not know that this dinner-party was to be memorable for us all, in more ways than one.

But whatever Fortune held in store did not concern us now. The dire struggle of armed forces on the continent and the threats to our country were obscured by the extent of our arrangements; and anticipation of the event to come coloured our activities, and our lives.

6

AS if to prove to me that her inheritance would make no difference to our friendship, Lydia made much of me during the coming days. She brought me a small locket from her aunt's collection of jewellery; she insisted that I should accept a fan which her aunt had treasured. Lady Deborah approved of these gifts, and herself accepted some tokens of esteem. It seemed that the happy days of the past were returning.

Philip had some leave due to him, and he was much at Charlecote at this time. He insisted that the three of us should make excursions as we used to do; we went again to Deal and walked along the promenade in the autumn sunshine; we visited Carey Castle. The three of us were gay and happy companions, it seemed with no cloud in view. Indeed, one circumstance added to my own pleasure, and gave these days a patina of gaiety I had never experienced before.

Philip became his old loving self towards me. Not when Lydia was present, of course; then we three were equal companions, equal to one another in affection and regard. But when we were alone ... He caught me in his arms, kissed me, assured me of his love and devotion. This demonstration of his caring went to my head like wine.

Sometimes I thought he had something on his mind; something of importance he wished to say to me. He paused in conversation, and looked at me earnestly, his blue eyes serious and intent. And then the moment passed, and we were our lively and carefree selves again.

He is on the brink of proposing to me, formally, I told myself. The words tremble on his lips; yet the time, in his view, is not opportune to make his declaration.

I wondered if he had spoken already to the General and Lady Deborah concerning his caring for me; sometimes I thought they knew; sometimes I thought their glances upon me were meaningful, as if they shared a secret I shared too.

Also, the preparations for the dinner-party were those, so I considered, in advance of any normal, formal entertainment. It was as if the occasion was going to be a special one; perhaps . . . Could it be that our engagement was going to be announced on that very night?

I awaited Philip's informing me of his intention; but he did not speak. Was the announcement then to be a surprise? Was this his purpose? To take my breath away with a fait accompli; did everyone know of his design, except myself?

I thought this must be the case. For a mood of gaiety gripped the household staff, as if they too knew that the coming party was an occasion of moment and happiness. It took me all my time not to mention the circumstances to Mrs Bagehot, and allow her to share my pleasure. But I decided I must play Philip's game.

Will Shepherd came to see Lady Deborah, and I was bade to be present and to assist the interview.

"I shall send Bruce Finnegan, my head barman, to be on duty in the entrance-hall and announce the guests," Will Shepherd said.

"Lance Pardoe, my second-man, shall assist Mrs Bagehot and Winifrede to serve the meal.

"I have already discussed with Mrs Bagehot the arrival and carving of the venison. The wines are ready to be transported. They will arrive a few days before the event, to give the lees time to settle in the flagons.

"Two of my best kitchen-hands will assist in the kitchens. I know that Winifrede is a skilled hand with pastry, and my wife has promised to make some cherry-tartlets which will not disgrace you."

At this mention of Will's wife, Lady Deborah raised her head. "How is Belinda?" she asked. "I would greatly like to see her, if she would care to call."

"I will convey your message," said Will evenly. "And thank you for your enquiry.

"She is in the best of health, and our son, George, is doing well."

The words were ordinary enough, and yet I felt that beneath them there was much meaning, unexpressed to myself. Then Will continued to discuss the matter of the menu for the party; and the awkward hiatus was glossed over.

When Will had gone, I pondered over my recollection of this man. Stalwart, powerful; a person of great integrity, I thought. No doubt he made a fine husband, and little George would discover in him a devoted father. For a moment I envied them their happiness, then other duties claimed me, and I put the matter from my mind.

The day of the dinner-party dawned at last. Madame Serle came early, bringing our dresses, which she had managed to finish on time. Lady Deborah's dress was of azure velvet, trimmed with silken fringe. For myself, I had ordered a sculptured stuff of pale green silk, trimmed with ruching and gold insertion.

I felt I had been daring in my choice, but Lady Deborah and Madame Serle had urged me to accept the decollotage. The fact that the General had insisted that I should receive an increased emmolument for my duties, now that

I was assistant translator to himself, had enabled me to select a pleasing material. The pale gold of the tracery shaded in the light, and faint fronds of greenery and flowers were shown.

As I dressed myself that early evening, and I looked in the mirror, I could scarcely believe that this was myself. I remembered how I had looked when I first came to Charlecote. That was three years ago, when I was sixteen. How time had flown! I was now nineteen; and soon to be betrothed, I thought.

I remembered my earlier self with wonderment and dismay. My hair drawn back from my face in a bundle; my clothes antiquated and shabby. My knowledge of the world nil; my expectations clouded with ignorance and apprehension. How different was the picture now!

I saw that the Kentish air and my settled life at Charlecote had brought colour to my cheeks, and brightness to my eyes. My hair, dressed already by Madame Serle's assistant, was mounted lightly on my head, with tendrils falling about the face. My hair seemed brighter, with more colour; brown at the rear, but with lightness about the face. I saw that my lips were parted in a smile. I laughed suddenly, unable to hold in check my gaiety and my surety of the rightness of life.

My figure had not altered, but my stance was different. Before I had been a little bent, perhaps through my habit of constant study, but also, I thought, because I was nervous in the presence of other people. But now, the fact that my new position as translator had been confirmed by the General, and my knowledge of the love in my life, and my future looming so large . . . All these things had given me a new confidence in life and myself.

And my success with Lady Deborah warmed me too; for this was the reason for my presence at Charlecote, and must be at all times at the forefront of my mind. Until . . . Until I became the wife of Philip, and resumed other responsibilities, I thought. Until I exchanged one mode of life for another; until my love was fulfilled, and we found our happiness in one another. I put out my hand, and touched my laughing face in the mirror. It seemed to me that nothing could go wrong.

How I would have liked Gérard to know of my good fortune! I thought. He would have congratulated me, been pleased. But suddenly, as I thought of my old friend of Oxford days, as I remembered the pressed rose which I still cherished in the pages of my lexicon, a slight shadow fell over my happiness. Then I put all misgivings from me sternly. And Aunt Betsey too, I told myself. I would take Philip to see her as soon as we were officially engaged.

I was busy from then on, assisting Lady Deborah to make the journey downstairs, settling her in her chair beside the door, and supervising the last minute preparations. The drawing-room looked lovely; with the chippendale furniture polished and new cushions sewn. In the dining-room, Mrs Bagehot had excelled herself; and the silver shone like white icicles upon the snowy glissade of the starched white cloth.

Everywhere there were silver vases of autumn flowers; the gold and cream of the blooms adding to the scene. Beneath the gleam of the chandeliers the beautiful and elegant rooms were shown at their best. I felt it a privilege to be present; let alone a coming participant in a major scene.

For as the guests arrived, it seemed that they too were in gay and expectant mood. It was as if everyone knew that some important announcement was to be made; and were deeply in favour, and willing to applaud the intimation. There was no doubt but that Lady Deborah and the General had told all their friends of the coming announcement. I felt my acceptance by everyone present was only a matter of time.

I checked over the guest-list in my mind, as I surveyed the now thronging scene. All the senior officers of the Regiment were present with their wives. The adjutant; the principal Majors, the loyal and hard-working captains with their ladies. The General stood beside the drawing-room door, shaking the hand of each male guest; bowing courteously to the wife. Lady Deborah had managed to stand for this part of the proceedings, and she greeted each friend with gaiety and genuine pleasure — I felt that the evening must be, in every way, an unqualified success.

Then I heard a slight disturbance at the door, as if someone of importance had arrived. I saw a man appear at the threshold of the room; but he was a stranger to me; he was someone I had never seen before.

"Captain Harry Delaney," Bruce Finnegan intoned in a loud voice. "The Royal Blues and Captain of His Royal Highness, the Prince of Wales' Bodyguard."

Captain Delaney inclined his head a little as if accepting the salute, and entered the room. And he was immediately enfolded in Lady Deborah's arms, and her voice rang out above the other voices of the guests, around us.

"Harry! Harry darling! My precious boy. How glad I am to see you!"

And she planted a kiss upon the Captain's laughing face, while the General seized the Captain's hand in a warm handshake; and between them, the two hosts drew the Captain into the crowded room.

I saw that Captain Delaney was very tall and thin; he wore a tightly fitting dark blue uniform with brass buttons, and a white shirt and neck-cloth. I learned later that this was the uniform favoured by the Prince of Wales, and which, by his decree, his personal bodyguard wore at all times.

His face was pale, a little tired, I thought, and was in direct contrast to his hair, which was jet black and worn without powder, which again I learned was a feature favoured by the Prince of Wales for his men.

So black was Captain Delaney's hair, I thought, it seemed that blue lights lay across the smooth crown; or sometimes, when he moved his shoulders, a haze of lightness, like reflected brilliance, was cast outwards from his head. His features were small and even, not prominent; his lips mobile and well-formed. His stance, as he joined a group of senior officers and their wives, was relaxed, knowledgeable, and sophisticated. His demeanour expressed a charm that was full of dignity and awareness. He seemed to bring an aura of the sophisticated circle of the Prince of Wales into the room. He had translated Brighton into Charlecote. He had brought the court into this country home.

He is a fop, I thought. I contrasted this tall and elegant figure with the General's stalwart masculinity, with Philip's energy and directness. I thought of the troopers of the Dragoons training ceaselessly either to repel the invasion, or to support the Duke of Wellington overseas. I remembered the volunteers drilling endlessly in the night airs to play their sturdy part. And here was this so called officer, fighting a vital war for Britain amid the comfort, safety and luxury of Brighton!

Bodyguard to the Prince of Wales! What did he do? I asked myself. Protect the Prince from the advances of Mrs Fitzherbert, or the reproaches of Queen Caroline of Brunswick? As if he felt my disapproving glances, Captain Delaney turned his head and met my eyes. When he saw me blush, a shade of amusement passed over his face. Within a few minutes, with Lady Deborah upon his supporting arm, he crossed the room and stood before me. Lady Deborah began to speak.

"Caroline, this is my brother, Harry Delaney. Harry, this is Caroline of whom I have written to you, who has been such a support and comfort in my life, and to whom I owe so much. Talk together. I trust you will be friends. Pardon me, please. My other guests call me. Edmund! Give me your arm. Let us allow Caroline and Harry to get acquainted."

Harry Delaney seemed amused by the situation, but his manners prompted him to be gracious. "I am delighted to make the acquaintance of the young lady who has been so kindly towards my sister," he said. "I regret I have not met you earlier, but my duties have been pressing, and have prevented me from visiting my sister at Charlecote."

Pressing? I thought. The gaming tables, the feasts, the dalliance of the court at Brighton! The war was pressing, but the Prince of Wales was scared only for his own safety. And the king . . . He was ill again, and needed cossetting, I had heard. What a good thing men like the General and Philip were in command in this war. Officers such as this Harry Delaney would need protection themselves, when the invasion came.

"You do not approve of me," Harry Delaney said. "Is it the brass buttons of my uniform? Do you disapprove of my service at the court at Brighton? I have met this disapproval before, particularly in the presence of fighting men.

"Do not forget, Miss Lancing, that the royal family need stringent protection at this time. The Prince of Wales would be a valuable hostage for Napoleon. The Corsican could bring our country to its knees with hard bargaining. The king is greatly misunderstood. He needs our support and regard to ensure a stable constitution. The bodyguard, indeed, serve a useful purpose. We all serve our own purposes in this war. And some more openly and in the front line, than others."

There was some hidden meaning in his words, which I could not fathom. But all further conversation and pondering was prevented for both of us; for at this moment Bruce Finnegan stood just inside the door and requested, in a stentorian voice, that the guests should now repair to the dining-room. Dinner was to be served, the voice told us. Please to be upstanding and this way . . . This way . . . This way to the dining-room. Dinner was to be served . . . This way . . . This way . . .

To my surprise I found that I was to be partnered by Captain Harry Delaney. And upon the arm of the Captain of the Prince of Wales' Bodyguard, I entered the brilliantly lit, and lavishly decked room.

★ ★ ★

I felt some bewilderment when I saw that Philip and Lydia were seated together, and that a mood of quietness, almost hesitation, had seemed to fall upon them. They spoke neither to one another or to their opposite partners, who were the adjutant of the Regiment, and his wife.

How I wished we were all three together, I thought. I imagined our merry conversation, our jokes, our pleasure in the preliminaries of this momentous dinner-party. I found also, that I was tongue-tied with Captain Delaney, though he did not appear to notice. He continued to talk to me, to tell me of his life at court and the activities of the Prince of Wales. It was only later that I realised that, in spite of his flow of conversation, little of moment had been told me. The Captain had revealed nothing of what he did not want me to know.

I noticed that the service of the meal was faultless. I glimpsed Will Shepherd in the hall, supervising the men and maids. Course followed course, with gracious precision. The enjoyment of the guests was clear. I could not help but feel that the party was a great success.

I observed also that the air of anticipation which was everywhere prevelant seemed to mount as the meal progressed. The climax of the evening was approaching; events were leading up to a peak, a point, some incident of importance and note. And I flushed, as I realised that this would be the announcement of the engagement. I looked at Philip, and I knew that my feeling for him was evident in my eyes. But he did not meet my gaze. No doubt from circumspection, I decided. But my conviction that our betrothal was to be announced at any minute filled my mind, and overflowed into my waiting and eager heart.

At the end of the meal, the General called the company's attention to order. He rose to his feet. "I now have a pleasurable duty to perform" the General said. "One which you have been expecting, and will welcome. I am about to announce the betrothal of two young members of this circle. Two young people whom you all know and like, and who have chosen to spend the rest of their lives together."

There was silence at these words, but a silence of such quality it was like a distant noise; like a sea upon a shore; a far off stirring of thunder. "Please be upstanding, ladies and gentlemen, for a toast. A toast to my young nephew, Philip Hellier and his future wife."

The company rose, their glasses charged, smiles and congratulations upon their lips. Philip, of course, remained seated, and so did I. I expected, naturally, to receive the good wishes and congratulations of the guests, while being seated. To my amazement, I saw that Lydia had remained seated, too. The General's next words were like a thunder-clap in my ears.

"To Miss Lydia Clement, my nephew's beloved friend, we offer our wishes for every happiness. Ladies and Gentlemen, please toast a long life and every joy to Philip and Lydia. From this moment they are betrothed, and their marriage cannot long be delayed. To Philip and Lydia! Congratulations. Great happiness. Many blessings. Philip and Lydia! Every joy. Long Life. Philip and Lydia! Betrothed!"

Somehow I had managed to rise to my feet, and seize a glass of wine. I remember, as I tried to hold it aloft for the toast, that my hand trembled, and the wine spilled upon a centrepiece of flowers. As I sat down, I found Captain Delaney's hand had covered mine, holding my trembling fingers in a close and composing grasp. I could not even look at him, I was in the grip of so violent a fit of trembling. I murmured some words of excuse, and rose to my feet and left the table.

The room was in a turmoil now, as the guests thronged around Philip and Lydia, shaking hands, the ladies offering them embraces and kisses. It was the matter of a moment to thread my way through this throng, towards the french windows, which were open to the balmy night.

I stepped through the threshold of the windows out into the garden outside. As if drawn by unknown forces, I made my way towards the giant elm. I stepped into the welcoming shade of the ancient tree, and covered my face with my hands. Only then would I face the situation which had occurred. Only then would I try to come to terms with the catastrophe and myself.

★ ★ ★

It was my fault, and my fault alone, I told myself. No one else's fault. Mine, and mine alone.

No one had deceived me. I had deceived myself. All the pointers had been there, all the indications of the evening's events, yet I had not seen them. I had chosen to ignore them. I had wished to remain in ignorance. I had deluded myself into believing what I wanted to believe. I had believed in an insubstantional lie, because this is what I had wanted to be the truth.

I remembered the first indications of my feeling for Philip. The palpitations, the flushes, the trembling, the loss of appetite. The classic symptoms of infatuation, of first love, calf-love, immature longings!

I had fallen in love with Philip because I had wanted to be in love. I had wanted to become betrothed and married — and indeed, this was the only certainty for women alone in life, at this time. I had longed for the certainty of total commitment. I had believed in its possibility with Philip. Because this is what I wanted to believe, I had wishfully supposed this dream to be a close reality. In spite of all the indications as to the reverse, I had deluded myself into an error and a terrible mistake.

I saw from beneath the branches of the

elm tree, that the ladies were leaving the dining-room now, the men were offering cigars and the port was beginning to circulate. I could see into the drawing-room, where Winifrede and Mrs Bagehot were plumping up cushions before the ladies arrived for their coffee. I realised then that, insubstantial as a shade or a shadow, a man had left the dining-room and was approaching the giant elm.

He was tall, and his dark clothing merged into the night. His hair too, dark as midnight, gave back no reflecting glint from the windows or the rising moon. He stopped before the giant elm; his movements were so noiseless, he seemed scarcely to be present with me. When he spoke, Captain Delaney's voice was low and level but with a cadence of concern and authority.

"Miss Lancing, you were distressed in the dining-room. I cannot allow you to stand here alone. May I talk with you? May I assist you?

"It was clear to me that the announcement of the engagement was a surprise, and a matter of consternation to you. If there is any way in which

I can assist you in what is clearly a private matter, please inform me. And I assure you that my services, and your confidences, will be regarded as confidential."

I began to recover myself, with an effort. "I assure you sir," I said, "there is no cause for concern. I was overcome a little by the heat of the room, and the excitement of the occasion." I could not bear to think that the sophisticated Captain should know of my gaucheness and error. Skilled in dalliance, as he undoubtedly was, he would regard my presumptuousness towards Philip's intentions as humorous and laughable. I could not bear to add another snub to an already ruined evening.

The Captain entered the closeness of the sheltering elm, and stood by my side. And it was clear that any intention to mock or amuse himself was far from his mind.

"I too, on another occasion, expected some culmination, different from the one encountered," he said. "The experience is sharp and painful. And leaves a dark shadow upon the expectant personality and the eager mind."

I glanced at him at once, and saw that in the faint light his face was sad and thoughtful. He did not elucidate his statement, and I wondered at the circumstances which had prompted this disappointment and its subsequent pain.

"So we are partners in distress," he said in a lighter tone. "We must console one another. Come, let me see a smile. My sister tells me of your gaiety and grace! And my own furloughs from duty are too short for sorrow or regrets."

In some indefinable way the presence of this strange man had comforted me, and had taken away the sharpness of my distress. I smiled at his sallies in the darkness. There was much to be learned, I told myself, about human consolation at the court of the Prince of Wales!

Captain Delaney laughed suddenly, a laugh not of amusement or derision, but of a shared moment of happiness. He caught me in his arms, but not roughly or harshly, with a swift and easy lightness, yet with unmistakable intention.

He drew my head back so that it rested upon his arm, and lowered his face to mine. He kissed me full and closely upon the lips.

When I drew away from him, panting a little, unexpectedly moved by this unexpected salute, he threw his head back again and laughed once more.

And in the light of a shaft of moonlight through the branches of the tree, for the first time I saw his eyes.

I saw his eyes in darkness, as I had seen them once before; when he had kissed me earlier, beneath this very tree.

I saw that his eyes were very light grey, almost transparent, almost to the colour of water.

There was no mistaking the matter or the person; there was no room for any doubt.

Captain Harry Delaney was the glazier.

7

THE next few days after the dinner-party were busy ones for me, as Lady Deborah fell ill with a fit of migraine and exhaustion, and I was kept close to her side and busy in her room. But I had much to think about in my few leisure moments. And the memory of my conversation with Captain Delaney remained in my mind.

"You are the glazier," I had said to him, when I had drawn away after our kiss. "I recognise you now. You are a courier from the front in Spain."

"I wondered how long it would be before you saw through my disguise," the Captain replied.

"It was your eyes which gave you away," I answered.

"They are a disadvantage in my work," he said. "Which is why I wear always the cowl of my habit across my face."

The figure of the glazier filled my mind; I seemed without words, and the

Captain went on, "I am told that you are the translator of the Spanish material I gather on my expeditions. May I thank you? The General informs me that your work is extremely accurate."

I flushed at this unexpected compliment for, as was the custom at this time, no outward commendation was given me for my labours and none was expected. I thought the Captain's encouragement both unusual and warming. I looked again at the features of this strange and enigmatic man.

His expression was sombre. "My leave is nearly over," he said. "It has been brief indeed. I leave for Cadiz, tomorrow."

A shaft of fear went through me at his words; as if I feared for his safety in his hazardous course. "Take care!" I cried. The words were blurted out, almost without my cognisance, and I wondered at myself, revealing my sudden depth of feeling to someone almost a stranger. He took my hand in his.

"Take care, Miss Lancing, also, in your own course in life," he said. "Sometimes I think your steps are as hazardous as mine."

I looked at him intently in the gloom. It was as if he knew all about me; that I was an open book before him. Yet our words had been few; and some of those at cross-purpose, and uttered in a state of misunderstanding. I had a great deal to learn about this man.

If we were ever to meet again! "When will you return?" I asked.

He shook his head. "I do not know. I have to report firstly to the Prince of Wales, this very night, before my departure.

"The Prince approves my work as special agent; and my appointment to his bodyguard is the ideal cover for these assignments.

"I have also a personal matter to attend to in Spain. But my commissions for the Duke of Wellington over-ride all others. To aid the Duke to crush Napoleon is the aim of our work, and forever in the forefront of my mind."

He had raised my hand to his lips; but he was abstracted now. It was as if his words had taken him already away from Charlecote; and his habit of the glazier's trade was awaiting to conceal him as he journeyed into Spain.

"Were you surprised by the announcement of the engagement, Caroline?" Lady Deborah asked me. She was a little better now, and was anxious to talk about the evening. "I would love to have told you before the event, but Philip wished it otherwise. He swore the General and myself to secrecy, and Lydia concurred. You three have been such friends, I felt it was remiss of us to keep you in ignorance! But you took it in good part. I saw you congratulate them later. And their happiness must have pleased you. It is a most suitable and happy match in every way."

Her words were painful to me; yet I realised that the pain was less than I might have expected. In some indefinable way, my conversation with Captain Delaney, his sympathy and understanding, had eased the misery of the evening in my mind.

It was as if the presence of his tall and seemingly elegant figure had granted me the boon of strength; a strength which had stiffened my backbone to carry on without grieving or self-recrimination.

It seemed, from the Captain's demeanour and words, that he had expressed to me the knowledge that betrayal is part of life, that errors in judgement are made by all; and that to suffer such reverses is the common lot of men and women.

To feel that I was not in isolation with my self-reproach and sense of disaster was a calming and healing thought. The Captain had done much to bring me peace of mind.

Philip certainly kept out of my way during the next few days, but during his hours at Charlecote we were bound, eventually, to meet. This encounter took place on the upper landing. It was a moment of privacy. No one was near.

"I am truly sorry, Caroline, that things turned out as they did," Philip said. "Sorry of course, not for Lydia, but for yourself. If you will meet me alone away from Charlecote, I will explain. I am certain you will see my point of view, and you will agree to preserve our friendship in the future."

I looked at him levelly. You are marrying Lydia for her money, I thought.

111

Do you love her, or is the thought of gain enough to make you marry her?

Her money will aid the dire financial straits in which you find yourself, I thought. For it was commonly said throughout the household, by the servants, that Philip was now in grave monetary difficulties. Tradesmen were dunning him almost openly; it was not a situation he could bear without drastic measures. And he had taken the measures, I thought. Aunt Hawkins' money would relieve his debts, and enable him to face the future again.

I could not bear to meet him away from Charlecote, and hear his excuses. As for future friendship, the idea was difficult to consider, let alone endure.

"You took things too seriously," he said, almost petulantly. "When you first came to Charlecote you were a bumpkin, straight from Oxford. No man had looked at you twice! My friendship went to your head. You read into it more than I intended. Why must women be so stupid? This has happened to me before!" He checked himself, then resumed. "It pleased me to see you respond. It pleased me to see you blossom under my attentions. But it meant nothing, Caroline. Nothing! You have a lot to learn!"

I stood my ground before him, and looked at him with contempt. I had learned a bitter lesson from Philip; I thought that he too had not yet come to terms with life. Only vanity and weakness could have prompted him to have treated me as he did.

"You also have much to learn," I said, and fleetingly I thought of Captain Delaney with his poise, his humanity, and his integrity. Then I turned from Philip and ran from the corridor and sought the shelter and solace of my room.

There was a southern wing of rooms at Charlecote, which had been shut up for some time. Surplus furniture from the Manor was stored there; some military equipment was kept there in readiness. Lydia came to see me one morning, with great excitement upon her face.

"But first, before my news, I must thank you for your good wishes, Caroline. Your goodwill and approval mean so much to me. I felt I could not get married without your blessing. But I know how much you like Philip, we have been such friends together, I knew you would approve my choice!

"Now, concerning our future residence. The General and Lady Deborah have given permission for us to renovate the southern wing, and make our home there.

"They have given us the surplus furniture, as a gift. And I have inherited many fine pieces from my Aunt. Thus, between us, we shall found a delightful abode in next to no time. Come with me, Caroline. Let us do a tour of inspection. I am truly longing to show you my future house."

Lady Deborah instantly gave me leave of absence to accompany Lydia, and we set out to tour the southern wing.

"See, it has its own entrance, Caroline. And tall windows which open on to the garden. From the big drawing-room, we can see the giant elm!

"And the staircase. See how beautifully it curves up to the landing. And all the bedrooms open onto a central area. It needs almost no structural alterations, save to make a kitchen and servants quarters. And a study for Philip! And a room where I can continue my drawing. And perhaps this room . . . "

A nursery, I thought, though the word was not uttered by either of us. I knew that Lydia loved children, and would, in time, long for a child of her own.

Talking volubly, we returned to Charlecote. But as Lydia closed the door on the southern wing, it was as if my pleasure in her happiness was contained and left behind. And a strange sadness and sense of fear filled my heart.

★ ★ ★

I was distressed, sometime after this, to receive a letter from my Aunt Betsey. She had had a fall, she wrote, and was confined to her room in St Luke's College. I saw that her writing was shaky, and the letter was without her usual forthright comments upon the Master, the staff, and her surroundings.

An unease filled my mind, and I

115

determined to ask for leave to visit my only relation. But Lady Deborah suffered a sudden reverse in health, and an urgent despatch came from Cadiz with much material in the Spanish tongue. I was suddenly tied to my duties, and felt I could not in fairness ask to get away.

One afternoon, when she awoke from her rest, Lady Deborah began to speak about her brother. "I did not mention my brother, Harry, to you earlier, Caroline. This was not from any wish to preserve secrecy, but because I knew he was engaged upon confidential and hazardous work overseas.

"But now that I know you are assisting in his work I feel I can speak freely. I am concerned for his happiness. In a personal sense, I mean. I care for him dearly, and his future is of great importance to me."

I waited, and Lady Deborah went on. "He formed an attachment sometime ago for a Lady at the Spanish Court. Her name is Donna Isabella LaCruz.

"I understand she is of outstanding beauty and has many accomplishments. She can sing, play the piano, make lace,

debate in public and play the lute."
(All things I could not do! I suddenly
thought.) "She is naturally high-born
and is the daughter of the high vizier,
at the court. Of course, she has many
suitors and her final choice of husband
is a matter of speculation. The man she
will finally choose is regarded as a man
who will be honoured, most highly, in
Spain. It appeared for a time, that this
man would be my brother."

Lady Deborah fell silent again, clearly
ruminating upon her brother's fortunes,
and the intricacies of the situation. "The
court in Spain is very formal," she said.
"Or it was, until Napoleon intervened.

"But as you will know, Napoleon
holds King Charles of Spain his prisoner
in Bayonne. And King Charles' son,
Ferdinand VII, is incarcerated too.

"Joseph Napoleon has been named
King of Spain, and general rebellion
has broken out in the country. The
position has gone steadily from bad to
worse.

"The confusion aids my brother's
excursions as agent. He can move more
freely; defences are down, information is

easier to obtain. But as for his personal affairs . . .

"Donna Isabella is still at the court of the newly proclaimed King of Spain. But the situation is exacerbated by the fact that this country, England, is of course at war with Spain.

"This naturally affected the feelings of Donna Isabella towards my brother. He told me that she was distressed by her unsettled position, and blamed the British for much of her plight. She told my brother that she was not now sure whether or not she returned his affection. His position as secret agent for the Duke of Wellington put a strain upon her loyalties. Suddenly, his courtship and their romance was under a cloud."

Lady Deborah stopped. "I pray for him often," she said. "I pray for his safety and happiness. Both these are of paramount concern to me."

She began to cry suddenly, and I felt deeply touched by her emotion. For she so seldom gave way to depression or despondency. She bore her afflictions lightly, so that sometimes I thought we did not know the painfulness of her life;

painfulness that she so carefully hid from us. She suddenly drew me to her, and as a sister will, she kissed my cheek. She fell into a light doze, and I made her comfortable, and slipped away.

★ ★ ★

The renovations of the southern wing went on apace; decorators moved in, stalwart troopers in mufti moved furniture and did repairs; housemaids from Charlecote began to clean. Lydia flitted from room to room in a haze of activity and happiness, her peach-like face flushed, her hazel hair in disarray around her head.

She had already asked me to be bridesmaid at her wedding, but I felt that this was more than I could bear. I had made some excuse and declined the honour. She was disappointed, but bore this in good part.

It was while we were in the big drawing-room one day, that I looked from the window towards the hidden gate and the giant elm, and saw the figure of a woman enter the gate and move towards the shrubbery which faced the house.

The woman wore a long cloak, and I could not see her face. Her figure too was hidden; it was hard to guess her age or station in life.

"Who is this woman?" I asked Lydia. For I saw that the woman was stationary now; she stood facing the house, looking at the windows from behind the shelter of her hooded cape. Her stance was still and watchful; her mien, frankly, was puzzling and had an aura of menace. I could not guess her errand, or who she might be.

Lydia came running into the room, her arms full of cushion-cases, and a painted shade for a lamp. She deposited her burden on the sofa, and hastened to my side as I stood before the window.

But when she reached the window, and we both looked outside, the woman had gone.

"You are imagining things, Caroline," she cried. "What unknown person could pass the troopers and reach this house? Come my dear, Mrs Bagehot has paid us a visit to see how the maids are progressing, and has made us some camomile tea. That will soothe you, Caroline. And now, I want your advice upon this lamp. Do you think it is suitable for this room, or Philip's study? And the cushion-cases . . . "

Her voice ran on, lively with hope and happiness, and the intensity of her desire to create a congenial and beautiful home. But I did not move from the window. I sought to see still, the figure of the unknown visitant.

Then I put from me all misgivings sternly, and turned away from the window. I responded to my friend's mood of gaiety, and set myself to share in her activities and her anticipation of the future. A future, I told myself, that could hold only happiness and good fortune for Philip and Lydia in their new abode.

8

THE next day a letter arrived for me from the Master of St Luke's College, saying that my aunt's illness had not abated, and that she had asked him to write and request to see me. I at once consulted Lady Deborah and the General, and asked for leave to journey to Oxford to see my aunt, who was my only living relative. The request was granted, and a carriage put at my disposal.

As I packed a small overnight case I realised that I had been at Charlecote for over three years, and this was the first time I had left its walls. I had requested no leave, and had been granted none; such were the conditions of service at this time. But I had accepted the conditions willingly; though now I regretted not having begged for leave before. When I arrived in Oxford, my aunt's condition caused me grave concern.

She lay in her housekeeper's room at

St Luke's College, very comfortable, and well cared for; but her health had clearly deteriorated recently. The Master had engaged a nurse for her, and I was told that the College would pay all the bills connected with her illness, and wished only to have her restored to health to resume her duties again.

I sat by her bed and held her wasted hands. Hands which had been devoted to the care of others all her life! I kissed her white face, and smoothed her now snowy hair. Gratitude and pity filled my heart. I did not let her see my tears, but these fell when I was alone.

The Master's personal maid had prepared my little room, and there in a narrow bed, wedged up underneath the eaves of St Luke's, I passed the night. And so, I fell under the spell of Oxford again.

I heard the bells chime, heard again the slither of student's boots across a quad, smelled the aroma of chalk and ink, saw the lambent sky and the spires which pierced the white clouds.

I remembered my early life in Oxford; my dear father; his students who had adored him, and who had been inconsolable at his passing.

I remembered Gérard, my first man friend, who had helped me with irregular verbs, and told me stories of Paris and Provence. And he had given me a pressed rose! I had it still, at Charlecote. Still in the Lexicon! But Gérard was an enemy now. For we were at war with France.

I recalled suddenly seeing him one night scale the high walls of this very college, and steal along the battlements towards the main rotunda. I remembered seeing his figure scale the impossibly smooth and high dome, until he sat at last, waving upon its lofty peak.

How the students had cheered him; how he had been punished by the Dean of St Botolph's — with detention. And then he had escaped from this barred study in the basement to appear, like magic, before them in Hall! He had been fined and incarcerated again; but this time he bore his punishment with good grace. And made up for his offences by extra service to the Dean.

I stayed with my aunt for four days, assisting the nurse and not venturing far afield. I was rewarded by seeing that my aunt appeared better for my visit, and after an interview with the doctor, I thought there was room to hope that she would recover ere long. When I sat by her bed before my departure, she said:

"Are you not yet betrothed, Caroline? I thought when you entered the General's household you would meet many young men of good appearance and family who would pay you court.

"Has love come to you, dear child? Is there some impediment? I cannot believe that during these three years you have not met one man whom you feel you can love."

I flushed crimson at her words, with their concern and perception. "I have been occupied, Aunt," I said. "I have several friends, it is true. But no one to whom I am fully committed."

"How beautiful you have grown," she said, and she put out her hand with wonder and touched my hair. "You had the potential, in your early days in Oxford, but there was no one to assist you, or give you encouragement.

"But now . . . I feel sure that soon

someone will win your heart. I long to see you settled. To know your affections and future are secure would be my greatest joy."

I deemed that my aunt was sufficiently recovered for me to return to Charlecote, though I made an arrangement with the Master to inform me of any change in her condition. And so I returned by the General's private coach to Charlecote, which was for the present time, I thought, my home.

For my heart was wrenched by leaving Oxford; and I could hardly set my face to my return.

When I arrived at Charlecote I found that Lady Deborah was in reasonable health, and she was glad to see me, when I entered her room. "Welcome back, Caroline!" she cried. "Bless you, how I have missed you! No one reads the classics like you do, and no one else knows the intricacies of the French tongue.

"But you look tired. Rest and become refreshed, dear Caroline, for I wish to speak with you. I have made up my mind upon a matter of importance, and it behoves us to find a quiet hour so that we can converse without interruption.

"How was your aunt?" her voice continued; but when I glanced at her I saw that she had fallen into an uneasy sleep, and I knew that her mood of gaiety was a spurious one.

It was two or three days before we obtained the quiet hour which Lady Deborah sought. Then one afternoon she bade me bring my chair closer to her bed, and she began to speak to me.

"I have decided to inform you on the matter in question, because I deem this the right, and the expedient thing to do.

"I have discussed this topic with my husband, and though he has his doubts as to the wisdom of my course, yet he has given in to me, and told me I must do as I wish. I have taken cognissance of his objections; yet am still of the same mind to take you fully into my confidence."

I waited until these preliminaries were over; Lady Deborah then said, "The matter concerns the General's nephew, Philip. And the events took place before you came to Charlecote Manor.

She paused again. "You must know that Philip is the son of the General's sister and her husband. Both died many years ago of a pox which carried many people off at this time.

"Philip came into our charge from his middle youth. The General and I have no son, or indeed any children, as you know, and so we regarded Philip as our own son, and treated him as such.

"It has been a pleasure to have him in our lives, and yet . . . " Lady Deborah sighed. "There have been problems.

"The General attempted to school Philip in honourable ways, and he responded in some areas of thought and conduct. And yet in others he remained obdurate. Our precepts made little impression upon his mind.

"He was gay and gallant with young women, yet underneath his gallantry was a selfishness we found difficult to understand.

"The General is the soul of honour where young women, or indeed any women are concerned. But Philip . . . He appeared to have a different code altogether.

128

"We received several complaints from neighbouring families that Philip had courted their daughters, and had then tired of them and dismissed them in heartless fashion. But a greater misdemeanour did not come to light until Belinda Bagehot came as housemaid into this house.

"Within a short time, it appeared, Philip had paid his warmest attentions to Belinda, and had seduced her upon a promise of marriage.

"Mrs Bagehot came to see me, in some consternation. Belinda had expected Lieutenant Philip to keep to his word and to wed her. Particularly since she was expecting their child. But Philip had refused to keep his word, and indeed, had repudiated Belinda. He stoutly denied that the child was his.

"The General was drawn into the affair. He questioned Belinda in my presence and we both formed the opinion that Belinda spoke the truth. The child was Philip's, and Philip had solemnly promised marriage to gain his ends.

"The General made up his mind at once. Mrs Bagehot and Belinda were people of the utmost respectability, and had no stain on their name, and expected none.

"The General ordered that Philip should wed Belinda, without delay."

And now Lady Deborah paused, and fell into a kind of abstraction. I paused in my listening also, and thought over her final words.

That the General had instructed his nephew to marry his housemaid, would take society by surprise. Yet to myself it caused no dismay or sense of repudiation.

They were so honourable these two, Lady Deborah and General Franklyn, they were so far above chicanery and any deceit, that no other course would be acceptable to them.

Many other families would have dismissed Belinda instantly, have hushed the matter up; have reprimanded Philip and sent him away for a while until the affair blew over. But the General and his wife had decided otherwise. They had taken the unconventional course, and had expected their orders to be carried out.

"But when Belinda came again to see the General and myself," Lady Deborah resumed. "She told us that she firmly and utterly refused to marry Philip.

"When questioned as to her course in life, she would not reply, but said she would make her own way without help from anyone at Charlecote Manor.

"The General offered her a sum of money, not in any sense as a bribe, but as a matter of humanity to tide her over her difficult time. But this she refused forthwith. We could make no impression upon her.

"She gathered her things together and left this house. In truth, I have not seen her since.

"But before she went, she made a surprising statement, and this is one of the reasons why I am telling you this, Caroline.

"Belinda turned to Philip and told him that she hated him. She hated him, she said, not because of the baby, but because he had misused her affections, had betrayed her, and had humiliated her.

"She would not forget, she said. She would in time take her dues. She told Philip she would be revenged upon him, in due course, when she chose to do this. When the time was ripe, she said, she would take her revenge."

The stark words chilled me, and Lady Deborah was also affected by the memory of the words and scene. She turned her head from me and I saw tears fall into the cambric of her pillow and upon the dark-brown tendrils of her hair.

She recovered herself with an effort, and resumed, "The General then censured Philip for his behaviour, and warned him that he must at no time repeat these acts of wanton dalliance which had brought him into disrepute, and disaster.

"Philip was affected by his uncle's words, and made the promise to be more circumspect in future. We have relied upon his word, and have no occasion to believe he has offended again."

She looked at me searchingly, suddenly. "I did think once, that you were attracted to Philip, Caroline, and I warned you . . . I cannot believe that Philip led you on, and offered to you more than the ordinary friendship of two young people who frequent the same house."

She continued to fix me with a

penetrating gaze; I trembled, I felt my face go white, I clenched my hands. But I did not reply, and after a moment she appeared satisfied by my silence, and she relaxed her rigid mien and dried her eyes.

So, I thought, I needed not to have blamed myself so harshly and totally. I had been the victim of a skilled philanderer, who knew no bounds of obedience or loyalty in his searching for his temporary gratification.

No wonder he had kept our so-called friendship a secret, when he was under so grievous a cloud; when his former adventures had been censured. Belinda must hardly have left the house before I arrived. And without interval he had resumed his course, deceiving his uncle and aunt, and toying with my vulnerable affections.

And now he was engaged to Lydia! What sort of a marriage prospect could she have with Philip? Why had Lady Deborah allowed the engagement, when she knew so much of the background events?

"We instructed Philip," Lady Deborah

resumed, "that only when he was sure of his feelings, must he court and make his avowal to a lady. And this he did, Caroline. He assured us that he had met the love of his life, in Lydia. And she returned his affections. It was a moment of happiness for Edmund and myself. We congratulated the young couple, and set our faces to the future — We shared their happiness, and they ours."

I bowed my head. I did not remind Lady Deborah that Philip had made no avowal until Lydia had become an heiress. Were they aware of Philip's financial difficulties? I did not know. Lydia was being married for her money, I was sure of it. Yet I felt I could make no comment. No word from me would advance any situation, I told myself. I remained with my head bowed, and spoke no word.

And now Lady Deborah roused herself on the pillows, and pulled herself upright. "I am telling you this, Caroline, for one purpose, and one purpose only. To protect Lydia in her married life.

"For naturally she does not know of this situation — How could she know?

She has been rigidly brought up not to mix with tradespeople. How could she hear? And Mrs Bagehot assured me that Belinda had told no one of the paternity of her child.

"Lydia is therefore in ignorance of what has gone before. And it is my wish that she shall be kept in ignorance for all time."

I looked at Lady Deborah swiftly, but her ladyship rushed on. "I have made this decision, and wish to enforce it. Caroline, I appeal to you ... Help me ... Help me to do what I wish ... Aid me ... Assist me ... Help me, Caroline ..."

Lady Deborah was now in the grip of a spasm of distress. She wrung her hands and tears poured down her face — I calmed her with a pad of lavender water upon her temples, and eased her back into a more comfortable position in the bed. "I will do what I can," I said. "Please tell me what you want me to do."

"Keep this matter secret from Lydia," Lady Deborah replied. "When one knows a secret, one runs no risks in conversation, or otherwise. Keep the matter secret from Lydia. And guard them both, Caroline, dear."

"Guard them?"

"I had a talk with Will Shepherd after the dinner-party," Lady Deborah replied. "He assured me that Belinda was well, and made him a wonderful wife. He had loved her all his life, he told me, from their childhood, and had always wished to marry her — He cared for her son as if he were his own.

"Yet he said she still speaks of revenge. He is trying to wean her from this viewpoint, and he believes her attacks of resentment are becoming rarer, now. But all the same, if in one of these moods she should seek to injure Philip, and through Philip, Lydia . . . I would never forgive myself if I did not try to prevent such an action, now."

"How could she injure them?" I cried. "What could Belinda do?"

"The wedding will give her opportunity," Lady Deborah said.

"The wedding?" I answered.

"Have you not heard? But it has only been decided today. The wedding will

136

take place on January the 22nd."

January the 22nd, I thought. In just two month's time! How swiftly, I told myself, our lives would change. For I did not doubt but that this wedding would bring many alterations. "How could she perform any action of revenge during the wedding?"

"She could protest," Lady Deborah said. "She could enter the church and make a disturbance and disrupt the service.

"She could point the finger of accusation and scorn at Philip, and spoil the ceremony. She could bring consternation and disgrace upon us all."

★ ★ ★

I was silent for a few moments, thinking this matter over.

It was true that this had happened three times recently, in Lyddford. Outraged and discarded women had halted the marriage service, and had loudly and openly accused the bridegroom of their misery and disgrace.

The proceedings had been resumed,

137

eventually, when the offenders had been persuaded to leave the church. But there was no doubt about the distress caused to the two families; and clearly, the marriages had started on a note of sourness and discord.

Lady Deborah clearly feared that this would happen at the marriage of Philip and Lydia. "I have persuaded them to have a quiet ceremony," she said. "It is wartime after all, and Philip is on active service. A display of pomp is out of place.

"But you will help me, Caroline, won't you? I rely upon you. I have no one else. I appeal for your help. Your promise of assistance will allay the anxiety in my mind."

"Of course I will help you," I said. "You have only to tell me how." I attempted to calm and comfort her again. "Let me ring for tea, and comb your hair. A little of that powder from Madame Serle will not come amiss! What would the General say if he came in, and found you distressed? He would be distressed himself, and you would not wish for that."

Unbidden, the memory of the hooded figure in the grounds of South Court filled my mind, but I put the image firmly from me. When we had had tea, Lady Deborah fell into a more composed mood, and began to talk again.

"So Philip and Lydia will be married, if all goes well, as I plan that it shall. And Harry, my brother, is in Madrid trying to persuade the Donna Isabella to change her mind and to become betrothed to him.

"I hope he succeeds!" she cried. "I hope he comes back to these shores an engaged man! I long for his happiness, as I have told you before. I feel certain good fortune will come to him before too long.

"And what of yourself, Caroline? Is there no man you yourself can care for? I would love to see you betrothed. I blame myself that I have not asked the General to invite some young officers to Charlecote, for you to meet! And you have been able to go out so seldom. I blame myself for this."

I soothed her again. How ironic this is, I thought. How could I tell her that my youthful affections had been ensnared by that same wayward Philip; and that Captain Harry Delaney was now lodged, both day and night, within my own mind?

I longed for the Captain's happiness, it is true. But there was a pang in my heart to think that this would be with another woman; and that his marriage to the Donna Isabella would take him for ever out of my life and my sphere.

9

TIME passed swiftly as we prepared for the wedding; Christmas came and went with little celebration it seemed, for the General was greatly engrossed with matters at Lyddford Barracks.

"Napoleon is massing the Grand Army before the Niemen prior to entering Russia," he told me. "The Duke of Wellington is still in Spain and has called upon me for reinforcements. No doubt he has some plan in view. I shall learn what this is in due course, without doubt. But in the meantime we must train more men. And I have promised to inspect the volunteers. We must arrange manoeuvres. And there are more despatches from Spain."

I settled to my work in the ante-room, deciphering the despatches from the Spanish front. The Captain's evaluation of the situation was in English, of course. But he managed to obtain a large amount of material in the Spanish tongue. I thought he must be an agent of outstanding worth.

I thought of him constantly; both as the glazier, and as the elegant and sophisticated member of the Prince's bodyguard. But his kindness, his perception and his integrity remained in my mind, and were a solace in difficult moments. Sometimes I thought I felt again the nearness of his body and the pressure of his kiss.

Once, at the bottom of an official letter from the Spanish Department of War, the Captain had written faintly, in long sloping letters, "Salutations to the translator of Charlecote." And an unaccustomed warmth and pleasure had filled my heart.

But I told myself not to delude myself again, and to remain cool and circumspect in the placing of my affections. I remembered my disastrous relationship with Philip; and also the personal errand for which the Captain had gone to Madrid.

It was about this time that a mood of exhaustion and depression overcame me.

My life seemed difficult; my duties an effort and sometimes without end. This feeling was not helped by an interview with the General.

"Has my wife told you, Caroline, that she intends to go to the wedding service in the church at Lyddford?" he asked me.

"Lady Deborah go out of doors, in January?" I asked. "And into Lyddford, which is well known for its winds from the Channel, its fogs and its cold!"

He nodded his head. "I have remonstrated with her but she remains adamant. Therefore, we must take what measures to protect her, we can.

"Will you see Madame Serle, Caroline, and ask Madame to make my wife a long cloak, lined with fur?

"If Madame Serle can obtain the skins of sables, this would be very acceptable. Tell her not to worry about the expense.

"I am not concerned about the cost, if it will protect my wife. And please do not mention this to Lady Deborah, Caroline. I want the cloak to be a gift for her, and a surprise."

I looked at the General. I saw that his

face was lined with tiredness; his eyes were heavy, as if he had not slept.

He is not an old man, I thought. And indeed this was true. I was to learn that he was young for so high and important a command as the 18th Dragoons, facing the threatened invader and supplying always fresh troops for the Duke of Wellington.

In addition he travelled overseas frequently, taking part in the Duke's military engagements, and rallying the men by personal example. He was head of the secret service too; with all its responsibilities and long hours of interrogation and evaluation. No wonder he sometimes appeared tired, and in need of rest.

Lady Deborah also, must be a source of concern for him; and the lack of wifely support at his side must cause him to miss the comfort and strength of a woman's presence. I felt suddenly overwhelmed with pity for the man before me; but I did not, of course, allow this to show upon my face.

"I am also deeply concerned upon the matter of security at the wedding," the

General went on. "My wife will have told you what she fears. And indeed, I sometimes consider, knowing the lady in question who might cause a disturbance, that my wife is quite right in her fears, and her determination to obstruct any intruder. And it is upon this matter, Caroline, that I wish to speak to you now.

"I have arranged for two troopers in mufti to attend the ceremony, and act as watchdogs. They have orders to stand at the rear of the church, to keep the congregation under surveillance at all times, and to remove anyone who acts in an unorthodox or suspicious way.

"Mrs Belinda Shepherd has been named to them as the lady in the case, and they are charged to escort her from the church, by force if necessary. But under no circumstances to allow her to speak or cause a disturbance."

The General paused. "My wife and I both think it would not be proper or seemly for the lady to be removed from the church by two men, alone, without another woman present. Therefore, I have to ask you, Caroline . . .

145

"Will you also sit at the rear of the church, and assist the troopers, by accompanying the party from the church, if this should be necessary?"

I was taken aback by this request, which I did not relish, and indeed it was upon the tip of my tongue to express my distaste for this matter, and to beg to be excused. But the General's eyes fixed on mine, the fatigue showing in his face, his personal distress at having to ask me to do what he knew must be repugnant . . . All these things weighed upon me. And I felt I must accept.

"I will certainly do as you wish, General," I said. I tried to make my voice as cordial as possible, to ease the General's burden of distress. But he was not deceived.

"I know it is displeasing to you," he said. "But I have no one else in the whole world to whom I might turn! Believe me, I appreciate your acceptance, and the kind way in which you have made your acceptance known."

I looked again at the General, and saw the look of strain had been somewhat relieved. He said, "I want you to know

146

how much I have appreciated your presence in my household, Caroline.

"You have not only eased the burden of my wife's invalidism for me in a way I would not have believed possible, but in addition, your kindliness and your understanding expressed to all members of the household at Charlecote have eased the working of the house, and have greatly improved the atmosphere of the home."

I was surprised and rather taken aback by these statements from the General; for he was not one to utter any facile praise, and beyond his first words of encouragement when I had come to Charlecote, we had not spoken upon any personal matter. But I knew he was sincere, and I valued his approval more than I could say.

The days sped by towards the wedding, which I knew I must now attend. For truth to tell, I had hoped to give some reason to evade the occasion, for I felt that for me, knowing all I now did about the circumstances surrounding both Philip and Lydia, the occasion would not be a happy one.

I saw Madame Serle about the cape; and by the utmost good fortune, found she had some Russian sables which had been brought in by cargoboat from Petrograd. "A good thing Boney does not know that his booty is being shunted out of the country," she said. "May his bones rot in the snows of Russia!" she added vehemently. "You will know he has divorced the Empress Josephine, and married Princess Marie-Louise of Austria. And they now have a son called the King of Rome!" she grimaced. "They call Napoleon the falcon, Miss Lancing, but the Duke of Wellington will catch him in a snare!"

The day of the wedding dawned bright and frosty, with a cold wind blowing in from the sea. Lady Deborah had been getting up a little each day, practicing walking and comporting herself ready for the ceremony. She was overjoyed by the gift of the cape, and it hung from her shoulders a torrent of brown velvet and rich skins. Her excitement and pleasure in the gift from the General was wonderful to see.

I wish I could record the details of

the wedding of Philip and Lydia in the parish church at Lyddford, but truth to tell I can remember little of it. I sat in a rear pew at the church, the troopers nearby, but there was no disturbance, and scarcely any strangers present.

The ceremony was a quiet one, for it had not been publicised. There followed a small reception for the two families at Charlecote, then Philip and Lydia left for a honeymoon in Bath.

So it is all over, I thought, as I allowed myself a glass of wine and a piece of cake. Belinda Shepherd did not contest the match in any way. Lady Deborah's fears were groundless. Belinda has forgotten the matter of revenge, I told myself. She has forgotten and perhaps, forgiven. Again I put the memory of the watchful figure of the woman in the shrubberies of the southern wing firmly from my recollection and my mind.

* * *

Lady Deborah had been greatly taxed by her excursion out-of-doors to the wedding, and took to her bed. The

General disappeared on his military occasions. Philip and Lydia returned to live in South Court, as the southern wing of Charlecote was now called. Philip was called upon to accompany the General overseas, and Lydia departed to visit her parents at Copthwaite Hall. So that I was almost alone when the letter from the Master of St Luke's College arrived.

He wrote to say that my Aunt Betsey had passed away, very peacefully in her sleep. He was arranging her funeral, and knew, of course, I would wish to attend.

If I would accept the hospitality of the College during my stay in Oxford he would be honoured, the Master wrote. I at once informed Lady Deborah of my bereavement, and asked permission to leave Charlecote for Oxford.

"If you could ask your sister, Mrs Sears, to come in as a nurse during my absence, Mrs Bagehot," I said, "I need not worry about Lady Deborah." For Lady Deborah had also developed a cough, and seemed in a restless and feverish state.

I went with sorrow to St Luke's

College. I saw the body of my aunt, and kept one night of vigil by her side; for this was one of the accepted obsequies of this time. The Master also honoured my aunt in this way. I slept a little in my room beneath the eaves; I knew this visit was for the last time.

Her funeral took place in a small university graveyard at Oxford, which was reserved for honoured servants of the colleges, for departed lecturers and dons. I was deeply affected and wept without shame. I knew the last ties of my early life were being torn asunder.

Back in the college, the Master asked me to prepare my aunt's effects for removal. It was then I found the sums of money.

I had sent an allotment from my pay, all the time I had been at Charlecote, ever since I began my work there. But my aunt had not spent the money upon her own needs, as I had wished. She had saved the money; and it was all neatly laid out in a box, still in its envelopes, still containing my loving letters. The discovery of this money affected me deeply.

I knew I could not keep it for myself; I had no other relatives in need. I took the money to the Master of the college and told him of its source. I asked him to accept the money for some use in the college.

The Master accepted the money and bought with it, I learned later, a leather volume with an illuminated frontispiece. This was presented to the Bodleian Library, in memory of my aunt.

It was a painful occasion when I said goodbye to the Master. I felt that I was leaving Oxford for ever. Suddenly, I did not want to go. I did not want to return to Charlecote. I longed to say to the Master, "Is there no work for me here? Is there nothing I can do to earn my keep? Could I take my aunts place . . . " But the words did not come. I bowed my head, and once again entered the General's coach, which he had sent for me. And so I returned to Charlecote. And to events I did not expect, and could not foresee.

★ ★ ★

When I arrived in Charlecote I was taken aback to see that Lady Deborah's condition had deteriorated. Her cough was harsher and more frequent. She lay in bed as if frozen into a block of ice.

She asked that the cloak which I had arranged for, and which had been a present from the General, should be draped over her bed. She stroked the skins with her hands, and seemed to draw warmth and comfort from its proximity.

"I think it would be a good thing, Caroline, if Mrs Sears could remain as nurse to my wife," the General told me. "Mrs Sears could remove much routine work from your shoulders and lighten the night's nursing." The General's eyes searched my face anxiously as he spoke. I tried not to let him see how deeply recent events had affected me. I did not wish to be overcome with vapours, or any other malaise.

But I felt deathly tired, and in the grip of deeper depression. Somehow, it seemed that there was no future for me. I could not see the possibility of any happiness in the way ahead.

I assented to the General's suggestion.

"And you yourself are wearied, Caroline, I can see that," the General said. "Could you not stay at South Court with Lydia for a few days? The rest and change would do you good."

But I shook my head. Something warned me to be on hand; and that great changes were ahead.

It was clear that Lady Deborah had caught a severe chill by going to the wedding, in spite of the cloak and all our care. She seemed to go downhill rapidly; her condition alternating between a sensation of freezing cold and torrid bodily heat. The physician appeared to be able to do nothing constructive for her.

Lady Deborah passed away three months after my Aunt Betsey's demise. Her going was tranquil, and she was conscious to the end.

She thanked the General for his love and care for her; she thanked me also for my efforts in her life. "I long for your happiness," she added, sadly. "As I long for the personal happiness of Harry. There has been no news of my brother for some time. Edmund says he is still in Madrid, but his despatches have ceased, the high command are concerned for him." She held my hand lightly in hers, as she closed her eyes. She breathed her brother's name as she began her last solitary journey into the unknown.

The whole household were stricken by Lady Deborah's death. The General bore his bereavement with courage and fortitude. I felt that I had been called upon to face a further grievous blow.

Lady Deborah had been more than a friend to me in my time at Charlecote. She had been as a sister, a mother, a beloved adviser, a close and understanding companion. Her passing left me with a sense of loss I had not thought to experience. Her departure from Charlecote was difficult to bear.

Her burial took place, privately, as she had wished, in the churchyard of Lyddford Church. She was laid to rest wrapped in the cloak which had brought her so much happiness. Her family and close friends attended the ceremony; but, as at the wedding, there was no sign of Harry Delaney. And no one mentioned the Captain's name.

That Captain Delaney was missing on

the Spanish scene was another source of anxiety to me. Yet why should I feel like this? I asked myself. The Captain had gone to Madrid to claim his bride; it was foolishness and self-delusion to even harbour his memory and his name.

After the funeral, the General asked me to go to the study, and bade me be seated before him. "I would like to ask you to stay on at Charlecote, to sort out my wife's effects and attend to her room, Caroline," he said.

"Also, the Spanish despatches are now coming through again, from a relief agent. We must give him all the support we can, until Harry Delaney reports for duty again."

He thanked me for my services, and I began my rather melancholy duties. But my heart was not in it; I felt that I had reached an impasse in my life, and that soon I must make a vital change. But what this change could be, and how I should go about effecting it, I did not know.

My meals had always been taken with Lady Deborah in her room, and Winifrede continued to bring me the trays, there. But the solitary nature of the room depressed me. It was peopled with ghosts and memories, and I felt I could not stay there alone.

As if the General knew of this, he gave orders to Mrs Bagehot that I was to have the use of the dining-room, and must take my meals there. Sometimes, the General joined me for supper, and we sat, one at each end of the big dining-table, taking our repast, and talking over the events of the day.

The General often asked me to accompany him into the drawing-room, and we sat beside the fire, discussing the latest despatches, and the confusing state of the war. At the end of the evening, the General bowed courteously, and went to the study. I knew he worked there, alone, late into the night.

When Lady Deborah's room was cleared, the General came to see me in my ante-room. "We have some urgent French despatches, Caroline," he said. "And I was wondering if you could help the sergeant translator with these. If you would care to stay on at Charlecote as French and Spanish translator . . . I will tell the adjutant. And we shall not lose your services!" he cried. "The war could not progress without you! The agents rely upon your accuracy so much!"

I felt the General was creating a position for me, at Charlecote, to assist me. It was as if he knew that I must soon offer my resignation, and move on.

One day sometime later, when I was busy in the ante-room translating a French despatch, a courier arrived. He was Lieutenant Bowles, a keen young soldier dedicated to his work.

When I had received his material from him, I asked, trying to make my voice as casual as possible, "Is there any news from the Spanish front? Have you seen or heard of Captain Delaney?"

"Harry?" cried Lieutenant Bowles. "I have heard that he is alive and well with a commission in Madrid.

"And he has been busy there, too! He has married a Spanish lady, a Donna Isabella LaCruz! The sly dog. I wonder, can he bring her home? Can he smuggle a high-born Spanish lady in his courier's pouch out of Madrid?"

The Lieutenant laughed at his jokes,

and I smiled too, not wishing to offend him. But the news had a shattering effect upon my composure.

When the young man had gone, I got up from my chair and took the despatches to the study where I wished to consult a map. I stood alone in the study before the window. I felt I had received a grievous yet secret, personal blow. I could not understand my reactions to the news of Harry Delaney's wedding. But somewhere, inside me, a secret hope had been crushed, and died.

It was at this moment that the General entered the room, and came to stand beside me at the window. He began to speak to me with great seriousness.

★ ★ ★

"Caroline," he said, "I intended to speak to you upon this matter in a few month's time. But I have today received orders from the Duke of Wellington, that he wishes me to join him as he prepares for the battle of Borodino.

"I am therefore obliged to speak to you now. Without delay. Before I leave

159

for the Duke's headquarters."

The General paused, then resumed, "I know that you have reached an impasse in your life," he went on. "One would be blind not to see your pain, and insensitive not to appreciate the recent blows which life has dealt you.

"Your health has clearly deteriorated, it is an effort to maintain your good spirits. You are obviously puzzled as to the next steps in your life. Yet I believe I can aid you in this dilemma, and attempt to solve some of the more pressing difficulties which face you."

I looked at the General attentively; for he was undoubtedly speaking with great sincerity, and the burden of his statements required effort and earnestness on his part. I wondered what his next words would be.

"I mourn my wife," he said, "but my military duties are so pressing and urgent I have to put aside my personal grief, and engage my thoughts upon my service to the war. The Duke of Wellington requires no less than total dedication from his men. I cannot fail the Duke. I cannot fail my service. So my period of mourning must be brief, and be overlaid by considerations of my occupation, and my efforts for the successful outcome of the war."

I waited still for the General to continue. I understood what he was trying to say, but I did not know the ending and point of his discource; and his private emotions, I thought, could have no connections with myself.

"I cared for my wife," he went on, "but we lived as brother and sister for a considerable time, even before her illness laid her low. I honour her memory; but it is as if she left me many years ago.

"Caroline." The General paused, and I looked up at him, and saw his fine brown eyes, the thickness of his glossy hair, his stalwart and manly physique. "Cannot you guess what I am trying to say?

"I shall be away for three months, in Europe," he said. "During that time I suggest you remain at Charlecote, rest quietly, and try to recover your health.

"Mrs Bagehot and Winifrede will care for you. I will leave you in their good charge. And then, upon my return . . .

"Caroline, cannot you believe what I

am attempting to say to you? Do you not know what is in my heart? We could be married, Caroline. You could become my wife. Will you marry me, my dear?

"I have cared for you for so long, so secretly, so intensely," the General resumed. "But I knew I could not by word or glance betray my attachment. But now that we are both free, it is another matter. I am most humbly asking you to receive my proposal. I am most humbly asking you to consider becoming my wife." And the General took my hand, and raised it to his lips.

★ ★ ★

I was dumbfounded, and yet, in a strange way, there seemed to be both logic and lack of surprise in the General's proposal.

And suddenly, the tears which I had held back for so long overcame me, and fell from my eyes. I felt my whole body tremble as it was racked with sobs; I covered my face with my hands, and would have fallen had not the General put out his arms, and drew me to his breast.

And so I stood there, my tears seeping into the braid of his military jacket; my head resting upon his broad chest. His arms were a haven in which I rested; a haven from the recent onslaughts I had suffered in my life.

When my tears had ceased I stood there still, standing motionless, still within the strength and surety of his arms. We spoke no words, and when I was calm, he let me go. But he still held my hand; and his grasp was like a strong and sure lifeline in a tempestuous and troubled sea.

10

THE General was absent from England's shore for longer than three months. It was almost six months before he returned to Charlecote. During his absence as he suggested, I remained quietly at Charlecote, and gradually recovered my health and my former spirits.

The General had apprised Mrs Bagehot and Winifrede of his intentions before his departure; and they both accepted me, without any words being spoken, as the future mistress of Charlecote Manor, and the future wife of their employer.

Indeed, I often thought that the General's announcement of our future engagement came to them as no surprise. And I concluded that the General's growing regard for me must have been visible to the staff of the house, while it had been unknown to myself. And I wondered for how long, since Lady Deborah's death, the General had revealed his intention concerning myself; an honourable intention which had been clear to others, though unrealised and unremarked by myself.

During this quiet period in my life, when I had recovered my health, I arranged for some redecoration to be done to the house, and some necessary repairs — particularly to Mrs Bagehot and Winifrede's quarters. The General had also left word with the staff that any renovations I wished to be carried out, were to be attended to at once.

So that suddenly there was paint and scrubbing, and new covers for chairs and new curtains at the long windows. But I did not change the nature and character of the house; it was perfect in every way. But beeswax revealed fresh beauty in the ancient wood, and a new spirit of happiness and anticipation permeated the historic place.

Lydia had now taken up residence in South Court, and she was a frequent visitor to Charlecote. She came in and out of the house as if it were a second home, and her chatter and liveliness pleased and uplifted me.

Philip was now serving in France. Suddenly, I noticed that a mood of gloom had descended upon her, and she was no longer her usual sunny self.

"What is the matter, Lydia?" I asked her as we took tea in the big drawing-room at Charlecote one day. "Are you lonely? Do you miss Philip? Can I assist you in any way?"

"A grievous matter has been confirmed," she told me soberly. "It concerns the inheritance from my Aunt Hawkins. I am afraid . . . There is not so much money available as we anticipated.

"The estate was entailed," she told me. "Even the house was mortgaged. After the initial advance from the lawyers, there has been no more money available.

"My parents were disappointed. Philip also. Philip's reaction distressed me. It appeared that he had private financial problems, and wished for some of the money from the estate to ease his creditors and clear his debts.

"I was taken aback by his reaction," Lydia continued. "I was unaware of his difficulties, and that he was in urgent need of money. After he had gone to

France I got into touch with my aunt's lawyer again, and asked him to make further investigations into the position.

"I could not believe that there was no more money from anywhere . . . I buoyed up my spirits, certain that more money would materialise from somewhere. But the lawyer wrote to me this morning, that the coffers are empty. Even a sale of the remaining furniture had brought in next to nothing. My inheritance has proved a snare and a delusion. It is a matter which is causing me anxiety and grief."

I comforted her as best I could, though I was taken aback by this news. "Shall I tell Philip's uncle, upon his return from overseas?" I asked Lydia. "He may be able to assist."

But I thought it rather hard, privately, that the General should be called upon for more financial aid. For I knew that he allowed the couple the use of South Court, rent free, and had done much to renovate their home. I felt sure also, that he still made Philip an allowance, as in Philip's bachelor days, though I was not certain about this.

"No, no, do not mention it, Caroline.

Uncle Edmund must not know about our difficulties. Philip is adamant on this score."

She dried her eyes, and attempted to return to normality. "How happy I am for you, Caroline," she said with a gulp. "To have found the man you love and to discover in him so much to admire, to know him so worthy in every way. I envy you, but you deserve your happiness. And Uncle Edmund too, deserves to find some felicity and comfort in his life."

I thanked her for her good wishes, and walked with her to the french windows of the room. There she paused. "I grieve to tell you," she said, "that Philip's attitude changed towards me when he knew that the money had run out.

"On his last leave he was cold, distant, as if he had grown tired of me. I fear for my marriage, Caroline. And I would do anything to please Philip and restore our former happiness. I pray to know what to do."

I watched her slim and elegant figure cross the lawns towards the entrance to South Court. Her head was bowed, and dejection showed in her movements.

Almost immediately, Edmund returned home. He was deeply affected when he entered the study, and saw me after such a long time. He crossed the room and took me in his arms. I felt nothing but gratitude and pleasure upon his return, and accepted his embrace, and his kiss.

It was now January in this year 1813, and I was twenty-one. Napoleon had retreated from Moscow, overcome by the savage weather as much as Russian resistance, and Prussia was preparing to sign a treaty of alliance with Russia. Edmund had been instructed by the Duke of Wellington to return to England and resume his former command.

Edmund and I were married very quietly, soon after his arrival at Charlecote. Lydia had begged leave to attend me; Mrs Bagehot and Winifrede were present as guests. The adjutant and his wife and other officers and their wives and daughters supported us. We had a small reception in the General's room at Lyddford Barracks, and then returned home.

My feelings were mixed. I had thought

of Harry Delaney on my wedding morning, and then had put the memory of him from me with resolution. I wished him well in his own marriage; as I knew he would wish me well in mine.

I knew that my marriage to Edmund was not an ecstatic espousal, a young girl's dream, a fulfilment of longings and secret hopes. It was a mature marriage, I told myself. (I remember I even looked in the mirror as I told myself this, and saw that I had now gained some poise; my hair was well arranged, my Empire line dress modern and becoming.) It was a marriage of adult people, I informed my reflection, who had passed beyond being affected by the first flush of youthful love.

But I was determined to make the General as happy as I could. I was determined to devote myself to his interests and his well-being; to give him the companionship and comfort he had missed in his former life. I was sure I could do this, and I was determined to apply myself to making our marriage a successful one. For he had rescued me from the slough of despond; he had given me his strength when I most needed it, and he deserved my unstinted devotion in return.

And now began for me a more settled, and a happier period in my life. I loved Charlecote, and I had also a husband who was devoted to my welfare, and the fulfilment of my wishes. In addition, Edmund was an eager and knowledgeable companion; he appreciated my efforts for his comfort within the home, and praised my conduct of the household. I was repaid by seeing his eyes light up at my presence; and by seeing his spirits revive and hearing his good humoured laughter.

To my amazement, I found suddenly that I had not only gained a home, but that I had acquired high social status and a definite place in the scheme of things, in Lyddford.

I had not given a thought to my position as the wife of General Sir Edmund Franklyn, but suddenly I found that I was given precedence before other ladies in Lyddford; that my opinion was sought after, my wishes anticipated. But I trod carefully this thorny and unaccustomed path, for I did not want to make any mistakes. The General's stalwart presence by my side aided me; and I began to hope that I could in time find some small pleasure in this social and public role.

It was sometime after my marriage that an unusual incident occurred. I had occasion to enter the study, and I found Lydia standing beside the desk.

I was surprised, for Lydia and the staff and visitors to Charlecote all knew that this room was out of bounds. "Why, Lydia!" I said to her, when I had recovered a little from my astonishment at her presence. "Are you seeking someone? What matter can have brought you into the study?"

She did not answer but looked uneasily around. "I heard that Uncle Edmund had returned home from the barracks," she said finally. "And I thought I would like to see him. I was passing the study window, in the garden, and I thought . . . There could be no objection to my calling in."

"No objection whatever," I answered. "You may call anywhere at Charlecote, save in the study. Which is private to Edmund and military personnel.

"Please come to dinner this evening if you wish to speak with Edmund, Lydia," I said. "He will be delighted to see you. And he will want the latest news of Philip. Have you heard from him, from the front in France?"

To my surprise, a flush dyed her face, and she turned and almost ran from the room. I stood looking after her, perplexed, and at a loss for an explanation of her unusual conduct.

I put the matter from my mind until a few days later, while in the garden, I was convinced that I saw Lydia leave the study by the French window, again. Yet I was not sure, and did not feel able to mention this to her; I did not wish to tax her unnecessarily with a possible breaking of the General's rules.

The spring moved swiftly along; there was no news of Harry Delaney, and I felt it was not propitious to enquire. Then one day, in early summer, I entered the drawing-room from the garden, and found Harry Delaney standing alone in the big and sunny room.

I saw his tallness; he was thinner than before. I thought his face was pale and drawn, but there was no mistaking his air of nonchalant elegance, his smile, the blue-black sheen of his dark hair, the searching glance of his pale grey eyes.

I was unprepared for my reactions at seeing him. Pleasure flooded through me; relief at his safe arrival; joy at his presence. I realised that I had worried deeply over his safety, that hearing no word of him had been a kind of penance to me. And here he was, in the drawing-room, close at hand! I felt the gladness his presence brought must show upon my face.

But he also was delighted to see me. His pleasure matched mine. He came towards me with a smile, and took my hand in his. He bowed over my hand, in a formal kiss. But his touch was like a catalyst that forced my feelings to spill over. I felt I had never before been so happy in all my life.

I schooled my runaway feelings to formality. The Captain also withdrew a little, as if he too had revealed more than he intended. "Welcome home, Captain

Delaney," I said. "It has been a long time since you visited Charlecote!"

"Too long. And much has occurred since I was here last."

I waited for him to continue, but he did not elaborate. "Caroline," he said, "may I offer you my humble felicitations upon your marriage to Edmund? I have just left the barracks. Edmund is clearly the happiest man in Lyddford. I feel I must congratulate you upon this transformation in the General."

I found I was blushing at this compliment. "Thank you. I feel I must also offer you congratulations upon your own marriage, and wish you every happiness that life can bring."

To my surprise, the Captain did not speak, but looked at me speculatively. "Upon my marriage?" he said finally. "But I fear you have been misinformed. I am not married, and never have been."

I was deeply astonished by this news. "But I thought . . . I was told . . . I had the news from a reliable source that you had married the Donna Isabella in Madrid."

"May I enquire as to who this reliable

source might be?"

I told Harry Delaney of my conversation with Lieutenant Bowles. Harry Delaney shook his head.

"The curse of the inexperienced agent!" he said. "Drawing wrong conclusions from insufficient evidence! Lieutenant Bowles deceived himself, and in his turn, deceived you.

"Donna Isabella married in Madrid, last year. Her bridegroom was a Captain Daufrey, a Captain in the royal guard at the Spanish court. It was a marriage emminently suitable to both."

Harry Delaney did not continue, though I longed to know the circumstances of this reversal in his fortunes.

That he too had been rejected by the woman he loved was clear. Naturally, he did not wish to speak of it. He did not wish to recount a record of disaster upon his arrival home. To ease the rather painful moment, I begged him to take a glass of wine. We sat down together, before the window, and continued to talk.

But I soon realised that Harry Delaney was going to impart to me no information about what I wished to know. Where had he been for so long? Had he been in Spain? Had he, by some stratagem, remained at the court of Madrid? What were the circumstances of the ending of the romance with Donna Isabella? What were his reactions upon returning to England? Had he, indeed, been in England for long?

Had he been at the court of Prinny in London or Brighton? What were his future plans? Did they include a future visit to Charlecote? But I stemmed this last speculation. I felt this could not possibly be any business of mine.

"You are clearly wondering about my errand, here," Harry Delaney said finally. "And I feel I must reveal to you my new commission.

"I have been seconded from the Prince of Wales' court to the service of the Duke of Wellington. And the Duke himself has given me my new orders.

"Caroline, you know of the network of agents whose headquarters are here, in Charlecote. You are one of our translators, and a gifted and speedy one, if I may say so. Edmund reports directly to the Duke on all matters. For naturally the Duke is the head of the organisation, and we are subject to his discipline and his orders.

"Caroline, there is a leakage of material from the British agents to Napoleon's high command in France.

"Several times the French commanders have anticipated our movements, and have been aware of our dispositions and plans. Naturally, this is a threat to the war efforts overseas — indeed, this affected the outcome at Lutzen and Bautzen — and is a threat also to the safety of Britain itself.

"The Duke has personally asked me to find the source of this leakage, and to stop the activities of the counter-agents. And this I am determined to do at all costs."

The Captain paused, then continued, "After investigation, I believe I have traced the source of the trouble. I believe that the leakage occurs here, at the headquarters of the organization. Caroline, the leakage of information is, I believe, taking place from Charlecote itself."

To say that I was amazed by this statement would be an understatement. I felt almost as if I had been accused of treachery myself!

To have the Captain and the Duke of Wellington suspect that a leakage of secret information was taking place from my home was shattering indeed. I ran over the security arrangements in my mind.

The house was guarded at all times by troopers, though they naturally allowed the staff of the house and tradesmen supplying Charlecote to pass.

When I had done the Spanish — and now the French — translations, they were at once inspected by the General or the adjutant, and despatched with all speed by courier, elsewhere. Where this other point was, before the intelligence was despatched to the continent, I did not know. But I suspected that the Prime Minister himself was kept aware of the work of the organisation and its conclusions.

But clearly, this next vantage point was

not in question. It was Charlecote which was suspected. It was from here, where I was now the mistress, that it was believed the leakage was taking place.

I had risen to my feet. I felt so perturbed by this information that I trembled a little. Harry rose also, and faced me.

"I have no proof," Harry Delaney said. "It is proof that I have come to Charlecote to seek. I shall visit here often to observe the conduct of the operation in this house. I am hopeful to discover the link between the agents here and overseas."

"If I can do anything to help you," I began, but Harry Delaney shook his head. "Do not take any part in this manoeuvre, Caroline," he told me firmly. "Continue your work as translator, and do nothing more.

"The French agents who are conducting this operation on behalf of their masters, are not to be trifled with. They are skilled and ruthless men.

"For a woman, inexperienced in warfare and without protection to take any part in this investigation may be asking for trouble. And I could not bear that any disaster should befall you. Play safe, Caroline, I beg you. And leave the entire investigation to me."

I felt warmed by the sincerity of his words, and the obvious feeling behind his warning. Again, Harry Delaney raised my hand to his lips and then, without another word, turned and left me. I watched his tall figure walking swiftly, like a black shadow, across the lawns of the garden. I heard the big gate close, and heard the troopers' cries and their salute.

11

I NOW had a great deal to think about, but my reflections were fragmented and uneasy. I had suspicions only to occupy my mind. But my suspicions were grave though insubstantial. And though I mulled over the recent happenings at Charlecote, I could come to no conclusion.

Edmund was delighted to see Harry, and though Harry was stationed at Lyddford Barracks, he came often to the house partly, I felt, from his own inclination, and partly to pursue his investigations. I knew that he questioned the troopers and other military personnel, but of the results of his enquiries he did not inform me. I sensed that he wished that I should keep strictly apart from this aspect of his life.

It was a glorious summer; how often when dire events face Britain has the sun shone upon this island, the sky remained cloudless and blue! Edmund was busy at the barracks and occupied in the study when he was at Charlecote. "Take Caroline into the garden, Harry," he would say to the Captain. "She has been lonely for so long while I have been overseas. And now I am fully occupied, as you know, and I cannot myself escort her. Go with Harry, Caroline. He can amuse you in my absence. And you can both tell me your news upon your return."

So it was, with Edmund's blessing, that Harry and I spent many happy hours of this summer together. The garden was well-kept and secluded, with many walks, trees, and the tiny arbour on the perimeter of the estate. It seemed that an unexpected bonus of happiness was granted to us both.

Some times linger in the mind for ever, with their undercurrents of secret happiness. So it was for myself; and so too, I suspected, it was for Harry Delaney.

We talked of many things, but never upon a deeply personal note. He did not ask me of the circumstances which had led up to my marriage to Edmund; I did not enquire as to the circumstances of his rejection by Donna Isabella, and his lost months in Spain. But we established a deep rapport without these personal revelations.

"Thank you for all you have done for the happiness of my family," Harry said one day. "You remade my sister's life and brought her only happiness. And now Edmund. His happiness matches Deborah's, though it is naturally of a different quality. And your friendship for myself . . . " He did not elaborate, and the moment passed. But his words added to my own pleasure, and the comfort and support I found in his presence.

When I was alone, I pondered the nature and character of my new friend.

That Harry Delaney was a man of courage and integrity I well knew. No one without these qualities would have been honoured with appointments by the Prince of Wales and the Duke of Wellington. And to move among foreign nationals as an agent, in disguise, and to conduct successful forays behind enemy lines, into enemy bastions of defence, and even into enemy headquarters, required coolness of a rare order. And then, somehow, to get his despatches home to England, and into Charlecote . . . Harry Delaney was an exceptional man; and well deserved the marks of favour he had been given.

I had sensed before he left for Spain the last time, that he was a man with an inner spirit of toughness and endurance. But now, since he had returned from Spain after so many months, with so much explained in his absence, it was as if I sensed within him a new spirit.

His endurance had, as it were, turned to a controlled initiative. Before, he had been dedicated to the war, but now, it seemed that he had made the war his own.

Something had happened, in Spain, I thought. Some circumstances, some events had turned the debonair Harry Delaney into a man of profoundly serious intent. I did not know what this could be. I could not envisage what had brought about this change.

And now occurred another disturbing incident. Both Harry and Edmund were absent from Charlecote during this particular afternoon, and I was busy deciphering some Spanish material. I had already completed my French translations, and had laid them on Edmund's desk in the study.

It was while I was passing along the corridor, in search of Mrs Bagehot with some question about the General's presence for the evening meal, that I thought I heard a small sound come from the study.

I opened the door, and stood motionless on the threshold.

For Lydia had again entered the study, in spite of my requests, and she stood now behind the General's desk, with some article, which I could not see, within her hand.

"Lydia!" I exclaimed. A sensation of fear, rather than vexation filled me. "You have been asked not to enter the General's study, and again you have disobeyed his request. Please, may I ask what you are doing here?"

"What business is it of yours?" she cried, in a sudden wave of petulance and antagonism. Her face had become flushed; tendrils of hair stuck to her overheated forehead, as if she was in a state of extreme tension. I saw her lips tremble over her small, even teeth.

"You are always against me!" she cried. "Now you have found your own happiness, you do not care about others! You do not care about my marriage. You do not care about Philip. It is left to me to . . . " Tears filled her eyes, but she dashed them away.

I knew her accusations against me were unfounded; I had tried always to see her point of view and make her welcome at Charlecote. But I was dismayed to see her still standing behind the General's desk, with the French and other despatches laid out before her.

"Why have you entered the study?" I cried. "What are you doing here?"

"I have brought Uncle Edmund a posy of flowers for his desk."

"Where is it?" I asked her.

"Here." And to my amazement, she moved slightly aside so as to reveal a small ornament in which she had arranged a spray of summer flowers.

This tiny gift had been placed behind a pile of maps. But now she held it in her hands and showed it to me.

I felt bewildered. I knew that Lydia was rather superficial in her viewpoint; that her interest in the war, apart from Philip's safety, was minimal. But as chatelaine of Charlecote, and wife of the general, I felt responsible for security in the study. Was Lydia so unthinking that she could not know the military reasons behind the need for security? Was she so unheedful that she saw no danger in her presence, no need for her to obey the rules which applied to everyone else?

But before I could speak to Lydia again, she gathered up her skirts and turned and ran from the study. She skipped over the sill of the French windows, and vanished outside.

I crossed to the desk. I looked at the papers arranged upon the desk-top. As far as I could see, nothing was missing. The despatches were in order. But the desk contained much military material apart from the agent's despatches.

And indeed, it was not solely the despatches that any interloper might be interested in. It was more likely the secret and confidential material which had its origins in England; which came from the military barracks at Lyddford, and which might pertain to the British high command's conduct of the war.

Lydia had held a package in her hand, when I came in through the door, I recollected. With a swift movement of her hand, she had secreted this package in the pocket of her skirt.

I visualised her again, as she stood behind the desk, as I entered the room. But I could not be sure.

I had not been sure, earlier, I told myself, when I had thought she had entered the study from the garden. And I could not be sure, now.

She had brought a posy of flowers for Philip's uncle. She had had a reason for her presence in the room. I had doubted her reason, but she had shown me the flowers. Indeed, they were before me on the desk now, in their tiny, gilt-trimmed vase.

Was I making more of an innocent girl's actions, than her nature warranted? Was I suspecting her without cause? I had been uncertain before; I could make a mistake again. I was filled with doubt, and told myself to tread warily. I did not want to hurt Edmund by any rather stupid suspicions concerning Lydia.

But I determined to be watchful and on my guard. I remembered Harry Delaney's warnings to me, not to proceed in any matter concerning the leakage of information alone. But I put these warnings from me. My suspicions were so tenuous, I told myself, there was nothing to share with anyone else. But some deep instinct told me to keep my own watch, and observe events.

It was only a little while after this incident, that I saw the gipsy enter the garden, and approach the door of South Court.

This family of gipsies were regular visitors to Charlecote. They sold pegs, besoms, beeswax and little geejaws of all kinds. Mrs Bagehot regularly purchased some household supplies from them; and I thought too, that Winifrede and the daily cleaning ladies had their fortunes told over a cup of camomile tea.

A harmless and pleasant occupation! I thought. The troopers on guard at Charlecote were always informed to allow the gipsies to pass. So it was without surprise that I saw the gipsy woman approach the front-door of Lydia's house, carrying upon her arm her basket of lavender and kettle-holders. I saw her knock at the door.

I was walking near to the shrubbery while the gipsy woman stood waiting on the outer-step of the door of South Court. I noticed that the woman was rather bent, dressed shabbily in dark and concealing clothes, with a kerchief drawn over her head and obscuring her face. She shook a little, as if some palsy had beset her.

The door of South Court opened, and Lydia herself stood on the inner-step. She spoke some pleasant words to the gipsy, and some small coins changed hands. I saw Lydia select the lavender she required, and two patchwork holders. I also saw her place within the gipsy's hand a small package.

The gipsy was now aware of my presence and my scrutiny. She shuffled and began to withdraw from the outer-step of South Court. As she turned I heard her voice, muffled, trembling, rather querulous. I felt her bright eyes upon me and saw her ingratiating smile.

"Thank you, my lady," she said to Lydia. "May God grant his grace for your pity to an old woman."

I stood quite still. For I knew that voice. It was disguised, overlaid with age and ignorance, but the tone and timbre were unmistakable.

It was as if the bells of Oxford rang in my head again, as if I saw once more the students of St Botolph's in their fustian, smelled their bread and cheese dinners, heard their cries as they left the long lectures.

There was no mistaking that voice, for it was engraved upon my mind and memory; it brought my girlhood back to me, memories of my father, my life in the College as a girl. And recollections of the student who was my first man friend.

For the voice was the voice of Gérard.

* * *

I had stood rooted to the spot, all initiative and direction taken from me by the shock. When I had recovered my composure, I found that the gipsy woman had quit the garden, and Lydia had descended the steps from her front entrance to speak to me.

"Caroline! What has happened to you? You have gone white as a sheet! Are you ill? Please enter the house and rest a while. I am concerned for you. This way!"

I removed myself as kindly as I could from her restraining arm. "Thank you, Lydia. I am quite recovered, now. It was just a spasm. Nothing serious. Excuse me please," and I turned to hasten away.

But Lydia would not let me go. I felt her hand hold mine. "Caroline, have you forgiven me please, for my ill humour of the other day? I don't know what came over me, to speak to you as I did! For you have shown nothing but kindliness throughout our friendship. I feel I owe you so much. Am I forgiven?"

"But of course, Lydia," I answered at once. "Speak of it no more. And now I must return to Charlecote." I turned resolutely away. But Lydia said, "Let me walk with you. I cannot let you go home alone." She linked her arm in mine. "You look as if a ghost has stepped over your grave!"

I shuddered at her words, which seemed to me to have a prophetic ring; to be almost an omen of disaster for the future. I thanked her at the door of Charlecote, and entered the house alone.

Once in my room, I rested a moment in a chair by the window. Mrs Bagehot had seen me enter the hall, and quite unasked she brought me an infusion of a new type of American tea. I found it quite agreeable, and it soothed my nerves so that I was able, at last, to think coherently, and consider what had occurred.

So Gérard was in England, I told myself. And there was no doubt but that he was fighting on the side of the French.

I remembered his words at St Botolphs, in Oxford. "To have a cause gives point and direction to one's life. I have a cause. My life will not be lived in vain if I can advance, in even a small measure, the cause in which I believe."

I had perhaps not taken his words

seriously, then. For students the world over are full of theories, heroics, longings for achievement, and sacrifice. But his words returned with force to me, now.

I remembered how Gérard had loved his homeland; he had never tired of telling me of the glories of France's history and attainments. That he would be a fervent and devoted fighter for the cause of victory in France, there could be no doubt.

On an impulse, I crossed to the bureau and took out my old lexicon. The rose lay still within its pages. A little paler now, perhaps, than when Gérard had given it to me. Its foliage dimmer, the thorn without a probe.

I closed the book, keeping the rose intact. Although he was an enemy now, I felt I could honour Gérard's sincerity and the integrity of his life. But the over-riding question was, what was taking place? How to explain Gérard's visit to Lydia, in disguise? All my suspicions and doubts concerning Lydia's actions now awoke.

What was Lydia doing? Was she taking documents from the study, and handing them to Gérard? Gérard was clearly a French agent. Knowing his resource and abilities, I thought it would not be long before the documents were in French hands.

Was Philip in touch with French agents? Did the French pay Philip for the information received? That Philip and Lydia were conducting this operation for monetary gain, was clear. I knew of their financial straits. There was no other explanation.

I rose from the chair in the window, and paced the big bedroom. What must I do about what I had seen and suspected? What must my course of action be?

And now I made a serious mistake. A mistake I was to regret all my life. I decided to keep, for the present moment, my information and conclusions to myself.

Harry Delaney had warned me. I had been told. I should have at once informed Edmund or Harry what had occurred, and have removed the responsibility and initiative to them. But I did not do this. I decided to keep further watch, alone.

Why did I do this? I have asked myself

since. Why did I not do the obvious and straightforward thing, and enlist the aid of the two military men connected with the home? Why did I decide to keep the matter secret, and continue to investigate, alone?

Was it the memories of Gérard? The memories of Oxford and my earlier life, which had been lived in such happy calm? Was I afraid of the consequences to Lydia, should I instigate official enquiries? That she was innocently taking part in this operation was clear. She had no malice. She did not know the meaning of the word treason.

Was I fearing to hurt Edmund? For I knew that if he suspected that Philip was in league with the French, he would be horribly hurt and furiously angry. Had I made yet a further mistake in my conclusions? I could have misjudged the passing of the supposed package, as I had misjudged the matter of the posy of flowers, before. The accusations were so serious, the penalties so severe, I dreaded to be the one to put the machinery into operation. I dreaded to make a disturbance without justification or cause.

So I determined to say nothing at the moment, but to keep watch upon future events.

Yet clearly, much was going on in the house itself. Edmund and Harry Delaney were often closeted together in the study. But they did not tell me anything of their deliberations. Why should they? They were clearly engaged upon matters of military concern. Yet suddenly, there were more troopers on guard outside the walls of Charlecote. And within the walls, stationed in the garden, troopers watched the house from the shrubberies or patrolled the perimeter, near the arbour. Unobtrusively, almost invisibly, the extra guards kept watch.

Gérard will not return if he thinks I have recognised him, I told myself. His disguise was impenetrable. His voice too, was altered and stressed. (And I had based so many suspicions and anxieties upon the timbre of the voice of an old gipsy woman! I chided myself.) But if he thinks I have not penetrated his disguise he will come again. Once. For I knew that agents were trained not to tempt providence too far. Twice under one disguise, was enough.

I tried again to visualise what had occurred. The gipsy woman had turned away as soon as she saw me approach. She had moved swiftly from the garden. I did not think she had seen my reactions, when I had been sure that this gipsy woman was the disguise of Gérard.

Gérard did not know then, that his disguise had been penetrated. He had recognised me, without doubt. I had not changed so much, I thought, from my earlier days at St Botolph's in Oxford. I was five years older it was true. But my features had not altered, nor my eyes and my hair. I felt certain that Gérard had recognised myself. But he did not know that I had recognised him.

That evening, Harry Delaney came to take the evening supper with Edmund and myself. We sat in the dining-room and shared our repast of pork stuffed with apples and sage, and a comfit of fruits and whey.

At the end of the meal when walnuts, cheese and wine were circulating, I was surprised to hear Harry say:

"I shall be obliged to forgo your

pleasant hospitality for a day or two, after tomorrow. I have received a summons from the Prince of Wales.

"The Prince is greatly concerned about his personal security, and that of Mrs Fitzherbert. An attack was recently made on the life of the Prince, and this has caused the Prince and the King great concern.

"Some madman of a Frenchman in disguise loosed a shot at the Prince's head. Luckily, the ball went wide, but it was an unnerving experience for the Prince and his companion.

"Mrs Fitzherbert fainted, there was great consternation amongst the body-guard. The Prince has sent a message," continued Harry now speaking to Edmund, "asking me if I could go to him at once to overhaul the security arrangements. And this I have agreed to do.

"I am under the orders of the Duke of Wellington, I know," Harry resumed. "But I believe the Duke will grant me a few days leave to attend the Prince.

"As the Duke's representative will you please confirm my actions in seeking to look into this matter?" Harry asked

Edmund. "I shall not be absent for long, and I believe this command to be one of priority, concerning as it does the safety of the heir to the throne."

Edmund at once gave his concurrence to Harry's plan. But I did not hear the words. For I was gripped by an unexpected emotion.

Harry Delaney visiting the court where there was danger! A madman's pistol shot could be fired again, and hit not the Prince but those who surrounded him upon his various occasions.

Harry could be injured or killed, as easily as the Prince. A wild dismay gripped me; a dreadful fear hammered in my chest. I felt my face go white, and I dropped my cheese knife upon my plate.

Both Edmund and Harry looked up at the clatter, and regarded me with concern. "Is aught amiss, my dear?" Edmund enquired, while Harry poured me a glass of wine. Both men regarded me attentively, clearly thinking I had been overtaken by faintness or other malaise.

I murmured some excuse, and picked

up my knife. I bent my head to my plate, so that they should not see my face.

How ridiculous I was, I chided myself. How stupid to fear an assassin's bullet, when Harry Delaney and Edmund too faced this, and worse during the course of their normal activity!

They were both serving soldiers, both used to undertaking missions both hazardous and arduous. Harry must have faced equal risks, during his time in Spain, of which he had still said nothing. And I knew that Edmund did not spare himself when leading his men. I had heard it said that he was always in the forefront of the fighting, leading, encouraging, inspiring his men to continued efforts. He was no general fighting from the rear, but a leader in both spirit and action.

At this moment it was my duty to leave the table, and allow Edmund and Harry to drink their port alone. But they came very soon into the drawing-room, where a jug of coffee awaited us all.

I sat still on the sofa, with my embroidery. But my heart was in a strange torment of fear and apprehension.

I was suddenly dreading to be left at Charlecote, with Harry gone. It seemed to me that I was going to be left to face the future, alone.

Edmund would be here true, but somehow, with Harry absent, it seemed that my chief shield and buckler would be gone.

The knowledge of my secret weighed heavily upon me. Gérard, Lydia; the package; the disguise. I should have told Harry and Edmund earlier, of what I had seen and suspected. I should tell them now! But somehow, no words came, and I remained silent.

They would ask me why I had not mentioned the matter before. They would sift and probe and then take drastic action. But I wanted to discover for myself the truth of what I had seen. Until I was quite sure the woman was Gérard, I would not speak.

As I was going upstairs to bed, I heard the two men talking in the hall, as Harry left to return to Lyddford Barracks.

"You will, of course, remain in charge of the operation, Edmund," Harry said. "The plan is laid, there can be no errors. I am sorry to leave at this vital moment, but I feel certain nothing can go wrong."

The two men continued to talk, as I surveyed them from the stairs. Both handsome, both men of character and integrity, yet so different! I was married to one, but my heart was deeply concerned for the other. I pondered this strange circumstance, as I continued on my way to bed.

★ ★ ★

Without appearing to do so, and when my duties at Charlecote allowed, I kept a watch upon the garden, the hidden gate, and the front approach to South Court.

The weather was beautiful; the days seemed long and filled with sunshine; the sky was arched with blue and freckled with white clouds. This gave me a perfect excuse for spending my free time in the garden. I even did my translations close to the window of the ante-room, in order to observe the movements of anyone approaching the house.

I knew the troopers had been

reinforced, but they were still deployed with discretion. Harry had gone without more ado, and Edmund still divided his time between Lyddford Barracks and Charlecote. It was an idylic scene, save for the threatening and unknown future. It might be possible that the gipsy woman would not visit South Court again; in which case all my suspicions and certainties would prove to be unfounded.

The gipsy woman entered the garden late one afternoon. I was walking near the giant elm when I saw the gipsy's bent figure approach the front of South Court. She carried her basket upon her arm, and in the basket I could espy clothes-pegs and other small articles carved from wood. She was stooping but agile, and moved directly towards the front door of Lydia's home. I observed her, and tried to note each detail of her appearance.

Her dress was old and threadbare but clean and mended. She wore still the kerchief pulled over her face, but her eyes were bright and clear. Hers was a rheumatic gait, her feet shuffling in ancient shoes. Suddenly, I was quite sure that I had made a mistake, and the ancient gipsy woman was all she appeared to be.

I had built a mountain out of a molehill! I had been infected by the scare of spies which ran through the whole population of Kent at this time. Everyone feared Napoleon. People saw agents in tradespeople they had known for years; friends were suspected, even relations assumed a sinister guise. I had fallen foul of this hysteria, I told myself. I turned as if to walk away and leave Lydia to greet the itinerant woman and her wares.

But something halted me. To this day, I do not know what it was. A turn of the head, a movement of a shoulder, a grip of a hand upon the handle of the basket. Suddenly, I decided I must put all my theories to the test. It could do no harm to discover the identity of the gipsy. If she was all she appeared to be, my theories were disproved for ever. If otherwise . . . I did not know. But I knew I must prove or disprove my suspicions and my doubts.

Lydia had come to the door of South

Court, and stood on the entrance-step, awaiting the approach of the gipsy. She wore a light shawl over her silk dress, rather unusual for such a warm day, I thought. But she was perfectly composed, and her attitude was pleasant and attentive. Her face was pale, and she held within her hand, her purse.

Again I observed the ritual; the handing over of a number of clothes-pegs, washing-tongs and clothes-hangers. Lydia paid the old woman, then drew from underneath her shawl a package. This changed hands swiftly, and was placed in the gipsy's basket beneath the rest of her wares.

As the old woman turned to go, I stepped forward swiftly from the shade of the tree, confronted the woman and barred her way. I said nothing to her, but one word. "Gérard," I said. "Gérard."

A flicker passed over the face of the old woman, and then was instantly gone. But in that moment I knew. There was no mistake. I recognised my former friend.

My test had shown me the truth. Had there been no small sign of recognition, no betrayal of identity, I would have accepted this non-recognition as evidence of my mistake. But my test had proved to me otherwise. This was truly Gérard. And in that moment, Gérard knew that he had been recognised beneath his disguise.

I leaned forward and put out my hand, intending to smooth the kerchief back from his face, in order to see at last the features I knew so well. But at my gesture, I heard Gérard utter a torrent of French; he raised his arm as if to protect himself. And then with one calculated and desperate gesture he brought his arm down. He struck me a blow upon the head and shoulders, and felled me to the ground.

12

I WAS in my bed at Charlecote. I could see the reflections upon the ceiling, see the curtains billowing a little from the soft breeze; hear faintly the cries of birds on the roof, the salutes of troopers, the distant sounds of the household. Pain ravaged my head and left shoulder. I closed my eyes.

I felt myself sinking backwards into an abyss of unconsciousness. Then with terrible, vivid clarity I saw the figure of Gérard.

I saw his raised arm, heard his voice. "Forgive me, Caroline," he cried in his native tongue. "Forgive me, my dear. This is a necessity to my cause." Then I felt the force of his arm as he struck me; heard my own cries of pain and surprise, and knew that I had sunk to the ground.

But in that same moment I knew that troopers had surrounded us. I remember Lydia's horrified expression as she stood motionless on the entrance-step of her home; her hands clasped in front of her, the goods bought from the so-called gipsy scattered around her. I knew that Gérard was seized, that he fought with all the strength he possessed before he was overcome. I saw the troopers hold him pinioned before he was dragged away.

But other hands had attended me, other troopers' hands had lifted me from the ground, had carried me into the house through the french windows of the study. Mrs Bagehot had appeared, and Winifrede. I heard their voices and their cries, felt their ministrations as they undressed me. I knew that Mrs Sears was summoned to attend my personal wants. But I had no wants except to lie alone in the darkness to allow nature to ease my suffering and my pain.

Edmund stayed with me for a long time. When I opened my eyes as Mrs Sears applied compresses to my head and shoulder, I saw tears upon his eyelashes; he held my hand with a desperation of anxiety and caring. I tried to soothe him. I remember I raised my hand and laid it upon his cheek, but I must have slipped away again into coma, for I remember no more.

That night, alone in the big bed, I dreamed with the vividness and intensity of my affliction. Harry Delaney came to me. He sat beside my bed and took my two hands in his. In my dream he bent forward, and laid his lips upon my cheek. I heard his words.

"That they should do this to you ... I would rather have undergone all the horrors they had arranged for me in Spain, than that one hair of your head should be harmed ...

"My beloved girl," he said. "My adored one ... " I listened intently trying to hear more of his words, but suddenly there was silence. And when I opened my eyes it was morning, and I was alone.

During the next day my head was clearer and the pain began to diminish. I also began to ponder the attack by Gérard, and the reason for his uncharacteristic action.

That my recognition had taken him by surprise was obvious. Yet he was not one to act in a panic. He had felled me to the ground in order to escape. He had thought I might call the troopers when I recognised him; to render me out of action would give him time to flee. He did not know that troopers were already on watch for him. And that even if he had not struck me, he would have been taken prisoner.

Edmund and Harry came to see me at midday. After I had expressed my pleasure at seeing Edmund, I felt the need to know the fate of my assailant, and to learn what had occurred after I had been struck down.

"How did you know or suspect that the gipsy woman was a spy?" I asked Harry. "The troopers were on the alert. Why was this?"

"Lieutenant Bowles delivered some correct information for a change," Harry answered drily. "He had learned that a French agent had been assigned to Charlecote. We knew that information was leaving Charlecote already," Harry went on. "It did not take us long to deduce that this must come not from Charlecote itself, but from South Court.

"This information was further strengthened by information given by the

Frenchman who had tried to shoot the Prince of Wales. I hastened back to Charlecote, with the Prince's permission. But I was too late. The blow to yourself had already been struck. But luckily, the agent was caught.

"I am told that you know this man who attacked you," Harry resumed.

"Yes. He was at St Botolph's when I was in Oxford, with my father," I answered. Then suddenly, I was overcome with returning pain. I closed my eyes. I felt the pressure of Harry's hand upon my own; then I struggled to return to consciousness for there was much I wished to know. "What has been the fate of Gérard?" I asked. "Is he captive, or has he been killed?"

"Not killed," answered Edmund promptly. "The British do not kill agents out of hand. They are tried first, and their sentence is then promulgated.

"He is a prisoner in Lyddford Barracks," Edmund added. "I have not seen him yet, but I intend to interview him today. Harry must return briefly to the Prince of Wales, so it falls to me to make the interrogation.

"But do not concern yourself with the prisoner, Caroline," Edmund said. "He will not attack you again. Or anyone else for that matter, I assure you.

"He is securely locked and guarded in the basement cells of the Barracks. He cannot escape. And when I question him myself I shall learn just who he is, and what is his mission and the extent of his knowledge of our defences. Rest assured, he will not trouble you more."

He will escape, I thought. No cells, no locks, no jailers will keep Gérard in an English jail, I told myself. Through the haze of my fast-ebbing consciousness I saw Gérard scaling the heights of the colleges at Oxford, heard the applause of his friends as he freed himself from incarceration. They will never hold him in custody, I heard myself saying distantly, as I drifted off into unconsciousness again. I wanted to tell Edmund this, but no words came.

The next day I deemed I was sufficiently recovered to come downstairs. I found Edmund in a state of grief and shock. It was clear, of course, that Lydia had been abstracting information from the study, and passing it to the French. Philip, now serving in France was, I learned later, paid directly by the French for this information. Under interrogation, Gérard had revealed nothing of the military details Edmund sought; but the documents in his possession implicated Philip grievously.

"He is my own nephew," Edmund told me, as we sat together on the sofa in the drawing-room at Charlecote. "My sister's adored son. That he would stoop so low as to betray his country . . . After all I had taught him. After taking him into my own regiment. After regarding him as my own son."

That Edmund was stoutly loyal to Britain's cause of fighting Napoleon went without saying; to betray this trust was of course, a heinous crime. He felt also the personal aspect of the matter. That his own relation had broken faith with his own proud code of conduct; that the leakage had occurred on the premises of Charlecote itself, was a double blow.

"Thank God that our apprehending of the French agent will soon be known to the French high command," Edmund continued. "They will know at once that no further despatches can be expected from South Court. Philip's term of damage and betrayal is over. Yet I must consider seriously my own course of action. He is my own nephew, and a serving soldier in my own regiment! Of the several courses of military discipline open to me, which am I to take?

"I have asked the military Notary-General to come to see me. He will arrive shortly from London, and we will discuss the matter in detail. Because Philip is a relation I must be stricter than usual to observe the legal aspects of the case. I can show no favouritism, but must be sure of my lawful course. I pray God to guide me in my decisions."

I attempted to calm him, but found few words to say. I found I was mostly concerned for Lydia. "Where is Lydia now?" I asked Edmund. "What happened after Gérard had struck me?" My words faltered, as I recalled the sharpness of the cruel blow.

"As soon as the miscreant was arrested," Edmund began, "Lydia knew that the package would be found, and the plot discovered, and her own involvement in it.

"She ran from the doorstep into the house," Edmund said. "She bolted and barred the door, and would not come out or admit visitors.

"I allowed some time to elapse in order for her to cool her disturbed feelings, then I myself visited South Court. A trooper accompanied me, and we made our way to her house.

"She admitted me without demur," Edmund continued, "and I asked her if she realised the full implications of her actions, and how dire the results of her betrayal could be to our efforts to overcome the French.

"She sobbed openly, in despair and contrition," Edmund said. "She had obeyed the orders of Philip, and had not realised how base a betrayal their conduct was. She begged for my forgiveness, and enquired as to my course of action concerning Philip. I told her I was still considering what disciplinary action I must put into force, but that I considered the penalties must be severe.

"Upon hearing these words she ran

into the hall. She snatched up her cloak and ran outside the house. I followed her, but was just in time to see her quit the garden. She was in no state to journey anywhere, and I sent the trooper after her. She ran towards the town and was soon lost to view."

I felt extremely perturbed by this news; Lydia had been more victim than traitor, and there was no doubt she had taken her reprimand by her Uncle Edmund, hard. I feared for her safety, for there were many malefactors about at this time; and it was not always safe for a woman to be unescorted and alone.

But Edmund's next words allayed my fears. "Later that day I sent a trooper to Copthwaite Hall, and he returned to say that Lydia was now staying there, with her parents. She was confined to bed in a state of shock, and could not receive visitors.

"I sent her a letter in which I instructed her to remain at Copthwaite Hall in the care of her parents, until I had decided my future course concerning Philip and herself.

"To the best of my knowledge, she is

there still," Edmund told me. "I do not think she will offend, again."

When Edmund had gone, I sat alone in the drawing-room. Yet I could not read or do my required mending; and my usual household pursuits suddenly palled.

For, quite apart from recent events, I now had an urgent personal matter to consider. I felt I must scrutinise and come to some sort of terms with my feelings for Harry Delaney. That these had undergone a change — or rather had grown in intensity to an emotion overwhelming and rather frightening — had been clear to me ever since I had begun to recover consciousness after my accident. The pressures of my new feelings were now sharp within my mind.

I sat quite still, trying to become calm in order properly to see my plight. For I knew that if I faced the truth, the truth would be a revelation I had not sought, and had never wished to see. If I faced the truth without flinching, my heart told me what my dilemma was, and must remain. If I allowed myself to face my feelings frankly, I knew that I must admit that I loved Harry Delaney with all my heart.

I loved him with a steadfast and enduring force and passion; with a warmth and sweetness never granted to me before.

How trivial and juvenile my feelings for Philip seemed now! And my infatuation had taken place so many years ago! I had been an immature girl in love with love; seeking a man on whom to pin my hopes and fancies. Philip had been near; and unscrupulous. He had taken advantage of my feelings; and my emotions had been bruised and broken as a result. But that was all over now. And I saw my infatuation as part of growing into maturity; an experience that could only highlight a mature love when time and inner development granted its arrival.

I got up from the sofa and walked to the window. How beautiful the gardens of Charlecote were, during this troubled and vital summer. A summer vital to the survival of Britain, and to the hearts of those who were connected with Charlecote. Mrs Bagehot entered at this moment, with a flask of milk for me and a slice of her ginger-cake. She believed that food heals many ills, and calms both body and mind.

I returned to the sofa. I considered Edmund and his love for me, and my affection for him. I owed him so much, I thought. When I was utterly castdown, without home, friends, or any direction in life; with my health almost ruined and my spirits sinking in despair . . . He had rescued me. He had offered his love, his protection and his home as mine utterly. Without strings or conditions. He had given me all of himself without stint or holding back. His love for myself was, I knew, the dominant personal emotion of his life.

And he was a man without parallel, I thought, in my experience. Honourable, kindly, thoughtful, tender. There was surely no end to the catalogue of his virtues! I had found no fault in him during the time of our marriage. I had sought only to be worthy of his love, and that he, in his turn, should find no fault in me.

And things had not changed, I told

myself, with the realisation of my love for Harry. I was still married to Edmund, whatever my private feelings were, whatever reaction had taken place between Harry and myself. We were held apart by strong though invisible barriers. And nothing in life could sever these bands; it seemed to me there was no release for us, ever.

For in a strange way, I felt sure that Harry Delaney returned my feelings. Perhaps he was on the rebound from Donna Isabella, I thought. Perhaps the still unrecounted ordeals he had undergone in Spain had prepared him for the release of love. I did not know. But I remembered his words when he had come to me when I was injured and unconscious. For I was certain now, that this incident had taken place. I even remembered his whispered and broken declaration of love.

I pondered the bleakness of my future course. If Edmund had been less kind; had I found fault in him; had the kindliness and peace of our marriage failed me ... I could at least have allowed myself to retain the memory of my love and Harry's caring for me. But I knew that this was not possible. I knew my course was clear. I must bury my love, deny my heart, and put the whole thing from my mind.

It was when I had reached this conclusion that Edmund entered the room. I knew at once that he had serious news.

"The Frenchman has escaped," he said. "No one knows how. But when the jailer went to the cells late last night, he found the cell empty and the miscreant gone.

"We can only hope that he has made tracks for France," Edmund continued. "And has gone to join his peers overseas. The whole regiment is on the alert for him, and the coast is watched. But he is a slippery dog, this one. I have ordered a reinforced guard around the house. We must take all steps so that he will not trouble Charlecote, again."

Edmund paused, and then went on, "The Notary General has been delayed in London, which means that Philip's case remains undiscussed. I do not relish this delay, for the matter vexes my mind both day and night."

Edmund came to the sofa and looked at me with concern. "And what of your health, dearest Caroline?" he said. "I can think of little else, except your recovery. Pray God you will be well soon." And he bent over me, and raised my hand to his lips.

★ ★ ★

The next day I decided that I must see Lydia; I told Edmund of my wish, and although he was not overtly enthusiastic, he ordered the carriage for me without delay. It was in the middle of the afternoon that I set out for Copthwaite Hall.

I had never visited Lydia's home before, and I was unprepared for the vastness of the Hall and its forbidding aspect. We had difficulty in gaining entrance to this pile; there was no one at the gatehouse, and repeated rings on the ancient bell brought no response. At last, a maid ran from the house and opened the gate. The carriage entered, and the horses drew up the drive towards the big front-door.

I was civilly though rather coldly received by the hostess, Mrs Clements. I had heard that she had a frosty exterior, and did not encourage callers. I knew I had not offended her, and put her reserve down to her habitual manner. Within a few minutes she called Lydia into the room.

I was shocked by the change in Philip's wife. Although she had been thin before, almost willowy, now she had lost a great deal of weight, and her clothes hung on her loosely. Her face was pale, her eyes lack lustre; even the still charming arrangement of her coiffeure was not a success, for her hair had lost its sheen and colour. She made a woebegone figure to my eyes.

Mrs Clements left us alone reluctantly, and Lydia and I sat on a window-seat, while a small dish of half-cold tea was served. When we were alone, Lydia began to speak to me at once.

"How are you, Caroline?" she cried. "I have thought of you often, and prayed that you were all right. That it should have been through a misdemeanour of mine, that you were felled to the ground! I have deeply regretted my actions, and I pray you forgive me for my part in the harm which befell you."

I had not thought of the incident in this light, and I reassured Lydia that I was now almost recovered, and for me the incident was fading into the past. "Uncle Edmund censured me exceedingly," Lydia continued. "I was hurt at the time, but I see now that I deserved his strictures. But Caroline, I assure you I did not realise the seriousness of the offence. And it was done, not for any gain for myself, but so that ... So that Philip could gain money to pay his debts," she went on. "And also, so that I could preserve my marriage.

"You, and you alone know of Philip's coldness to me when last he was on leave. His disappointment in me, my fear that our marriage was falling asunder ... I assure you, only the wish to preserve our happiness made me party to Philip's plan. Only the wish to preserve his love tempted me to play my part in what I know now is a treasonable act."

"Please do not be upset, Lydia," I told my friend. I felt deeply touched by this recital of her troubles; I thought she seemed better for unburdening herself to me. "And please, Caroline," Lydia continued, "will you ask Uncle Edmund if I may return to South Court? I long for my own home again. I seem not to be able to find any ease or comfort here." And she looked around her at the big room with its ugly and uncomfortable furnishings. It was a warm day, but even the air of the room was chill.

I remembered Lydia telling me a long time ago of her parents' disappointment in her legacy; it was clear there was little of home life or pleasure in this gaunt dwelling, with her remote and reserved relations. I assured her that I would consult Edmund, and see what I could do.

"I fear for her health in that cold place," I told Edmund upon my return. "Her parents have withdrawn from her, the world and one another. I beg you not to keep her there.

"I feel sure she will live quietly at South Court if you will grant her to return," I assured Edmund. "She will not transgress further. She loves her home, and you also, her Uncle Edmund. She told me to give you her felicitations and regards."

So Edmund relented, and Lydia returned to South Court. I welcomed her eagerly, and took in flowers, fruit, and a pie baked by Mrs Bagehot. Lydia's joy at being home again was touching to see, and I shared in her relief and happiness.

If we could have seen the future, it would have given us thought to pause. But we looked from the window of South Court now, and felt we had gained a reprieve. We did not know it was a reprieve before a more stringent sentence would befall. We did not know what the future held, or we could not have lived through this happier present in our lives.

★ ★ ★

That evening Edmund spoke with great seriousness to Harry, who had now returned from the court at London.

"You will know that I have today had discussions with the Notary General from Whitehall, concerning Philip, and I can see no way to finality in this matter save by a strict adherence to the fullest letter of the law.

"I have therefore decided to inform the high command of the Duke of Wellington of the offence committed by my nephew, Philip Hellier. He must be apprehended, arrested, and taken into custody by the military police. He must face the customary court martial and pay the exact penalty for treason with his future, and his life."

I had never doubted but that Edmund would finally come to this conclusion concerning Philip. Indeed, I knew he had made up his mind to his course before the arrival of the Notary General, and their discussions had been on legal matters only. Knowing Edmund, I was certain he would not spare a relation the penalty he would have demanded of any other soldier. Philip had committed the treasonable offence; he must pay for his betrayal of his country with his life.

"I therefore intend to have him recalled from France to Lyddford Barracks. I will ask the Duke of Wellington to sanction an independent tribunal to try and sentence him, here."

Harry Delaney had taken the evening supper with us, as he did frequently when he was in Lyddford. He did not answer the General at once, but appeared thoughtful. Finally, he said:

"I beg you not to be too hasty in this matter, sir." Involuntarily, he had adopted a more formal tone, as if they were already in the barracks. Their easy companionship had been put aside. "As you know, I have counselled caution from the beginning. I think you will gain less not more by precipitate action. I beg you to review the salient factors in this case."

"Precipitate action!" cried Edmund. "I have only countenanced the delay because of Philip's inability to do further harm! And what is there to review? The matter is finished and closed as far as I am concerned. When it passes out of my hands, its importance for me will be over. I am determined that military law must take its course."

"In due time, General," Harry Delaney said. "But will you consider another aspect of this case? I have spent much time upon this matter, and wish to put my conclusions before you.

"Philip's offence was heinous, but what are now the results? I personally examined past despatches, and from those missing was able to deduce the nature of the information supplied to the French.

"Most of that information concerned the troops stationed here, and deployed in France. It was an easy matter to issue fresh information and advise altered commands, so that these former instructions were not carried out. This I did, as you know, and I am assured that the former orders were annulled.

"It is true that the Duke of Wellington, being engaged at Vittoria, has not been told the details of this case. And for the moment I advise that the details be not revealed. Surely at the moment it is not necessary to disclose the traitor's identity? For the Duke to be informed that the miscreant has been apprehended, and his betrayal halted, is assuredly enough. In fact, I believe you will lose more than you will gain if you reveal Philip's name."

"What do you mean?" Edmund cried. "I am at a loss to follow your reasoning. Speak clearly to me, in specifics. I am not a woman who must be prepared with fine words!"

"The Duke of Wellington suspected that the leak in security originated in Charlecote," Harry answered. "He could accept that. But for the Duke to know that your own nephew was the traitor, and a lieutenant in the 18th Dragoons at that . . . I believe this would prove too much for him to swallow without strong reaction. He would consider the security of his latest operation would be in question. He would decline to visit Charlecote, as he has promised to do. And you know that this would be a hinderance to the success of the coming missions of the corps of intelligence."

Harry halted, and his words exploded like a firecracker in the quiet room. "The Duke of Wellington to visit Charlecote!" I cried. "When is this to be? Please tell me! The Duke of Wellington coming here!"

"I will give you all the details in due time, my dear," said Edmund calmly. "But in the meantime, please continue, Harry."

"I suggest that the identity of the traitor is kept secret until after the Duke of Wellington's visit," Harry said. "Later, when the matters under review are concluded, Philip's identity can be revealed.

"This is entirely within your jurisdiction to do, sir. You are the head of Intelligence. You can withhold or release information as you evaluate its importance to the winning of the war. I strongly advise you to take the broader view, and consider the vital discussions to be held during the Duke's visit. I will support your decision as security investigator in this matter. After all, the winning of the war and the success of the next mission of the corps of intelligence must be the important concerns for us all at the present time.

"When the Duke's visit is over," Harry resumed, "and the important questions are solved, the Duke will move away from Charlecote, and Philip's guilt will not concern him so directly. He will see it as a matter of personal grief to yourself, sir, rather than as a threat to the safety of his military objectives.

"Therefore I beg you, keep silent concerning Philip's betrayal until after the Duke's visit. As you yourself have said, Philip cannot harm the British cause more, for we have cut off the source of his supply of information. He is quite immoblised in his designs. Leave him where he is, in battle, facing the French. You can arrange his recall after the Duke's visit, and his court martial can take place in relative privacy. Surely a consideration of vital consequence to us all."

"Please consider Lydia!" I cried, for I had followed Harry's reasoning closely. "I fear for her health. She cannot take another shock so soon after the first. Philip's recall and court martial would be too much for her, I am certain. May I ask you to take into account her feelings and her health. She is living quietly at South Court, and needs a space of time in which to recover."

"I cannot take personal and family matters into consideration, now," Edmund replied kindly though firmly. "Only military matters can sway my judgment. And these considerations Harry has put before me.

"It is true the Duke's visit is the most important circumstance in our lives at the present moment," Edmund continued thoughtfully. "The Duke's safety and wellbeing while under our roof must be our prime regard.

"I could not bear to think that the Duke's peace of mind was threatened and his mission jeopardised by news of Philip's error and court martial. Yes, I see the force of your arguments. I will do what you suggest, Harry. I will hold the matter in abeyance at the present time, and proceed with Philip's deserts after the Duke's departure.

"And now my dear Caroline," said Edmund, turning to me. "I do not need to tell you that this is a matter of the utmost secrecy. Please guard the knowledge you have gained this evening, as if it were your life."

I assented without hesitation. But I sat still as if in a trance. Scarcely believing what I had been told. That the Duke of Wellington was to be our guest; the Iron Duke himself was to visit my home.

13

"THE date of the Duke's arrival is entirely at the Duke's discretion," Edmund told me later. "He has defeated the French in Spain at Vittoria, and Austria has entered the war. But I know the Duke plans to move ahead without surcease. We must allow him to set his own date of arrival.

"The Duke wishes to meet the twelve agents of his own personal network of intelligence. He wishes to thank these men individually. And also to commission them upon an operation in the future. An operation, preceding a battle, which will be of vital importance to this country, and the continent of Europe itself.

"Do not be distressed, Caroline," Edmund added. "I will give you as much notice of the Duke's arrival at Charlecote, as possible. But the whole operation must be shrouded in secrecy. Bear this in mind, my dear. The safety of the Duke may depend upon everyone concerned keeping their silence. Let the Duke find no fault in us, regarding this."

I set to, with Mrs Bagehot, to spruce the furnishings of the house. Yet everything was so clean and well-tended, there was truly little improvement to be made. Mrs Bagehot was mystified by these activities. It seemed there was little for me to do but wait for the date of the Duke's arrival; and learn then what was required of the household for the Duke's welfare and comfort, while he was under our roof.

I continued to visit Lydia, for she was still under a kind of voluntary house-arrest, which Edmund insisted should be enforced.

One day, I thought she seemed more depressed than usual. She said to me, "I am so worried, Caroline. I think I am having hallucinations. I keep seeing the figure of a woman in the garden. She moves in the shrubberies and beneath the elm trees. I see her quite clearly for one minute. But when I look again, she has gone.

"Tell me, what can be the explanation of this? Is there a woman? Or is my sight playing tricks with me? What do you advise? What can be done in the matter?"

"Do you believe you know this woman?" I asked.

She hesitated. "I think it is Belinda Bagehot, who used to work as housemaid for Lady Deborah. Do you remember? But no. It was before your time, Caroline. I believe it is she.

"And yet, I cannot truly suppose that Belinda would behave in such a manner. She is married now to Will Shepherd. And has a settled marriage and a position in Lyddford, as wife of the respected innkeeper. What could be her purpose in playing such a trick? It seems pointless and strange in the extreme."

"I have seen no woman in the garden, Lydia," I assured her, and this was true. "But I will keep watch on your behalf, and see if I can find some explanation for this matter.

"In the meantime, please rest as much as you can. Are you eating enough? Look, I have brought you some fromety and a jar of preserve, and Uncle Edmund has sent you a bottle of wine." Yes,

Edmund had relented enough to send Lydia a bottle of dry sack. He was more concerned for her happiness than he would admit.

I kept a constant watch on the garden (so far as I was able without being conspicuous to Mrs Bagehot and Winifrede and the guarding troopers) and one afternoon, I thought I saw an unusual movement in the shrubberies which faced South Court.

I drew my shawl about my shoulders, and stepped out of the french window into the garden. I walked, with as much haste as was decently possible, to where I had seen the leaves of the deciduous shrubs move.

Sure enough, in the tiny narrow path behind the shrubbery I found the figure of a woman. She wore a long grey cloak with a hood, but there was no mistaking her face and stance. This was indeed the former Belinda Bagehot, keeping watch upon South Court.

"Good afternoon Mrs Shepherd," I said pleasantly. "May I ask your errand in the garden this afternoon?"

She was surprised by my sudden

appearance, and question. She became flustered, and replied, "I have come to visit my aunt, Mrs Bagehot. She is expecting me for tea."

I knew this was false, for Mrs Bagehot had already gone into Lyddford on a shopping errand for the household. I continued, "Then may I enquire as to why you are using the path in the shrubbery? As you will know, this leads only to the arbour, and not to the house."

"I felt in need of air," Belinda Shepherd replied. "A sudden faintness assailed me."

"May I assist you to the house?" I enquired, and Belinda answered, "Thank you no, Lady Franklyn. I think I will return home."

It was at this moment that I saw the figure of Lydia emerge from the front-door of South Court. She sped across the lawns and entered the shrubbery.

I saw that she was in the grip of some strong emotion; even excitement. She faced Belinda Shepherd in a confrontation of anger and pride. Her eyes blazed, and colour flamed in her cheeks. Her voice was almost stifled with her emotion as she cried:

"How dare you trespass again in my garden! Your continual spying is an embarrassment and an affront to me. Pray leave the confines of my house! I cannot bear to see you in my garden, again."

I saw that Belinda Shepherd was taken aback by this outburst. "I have done no harm," she said. "It is the custom at Charlecote for servants to walk in the shrubbery."

"You are a servant at Charlecote no longer," Lydia replied. "Please quit these premises, and do not return."

And now Belinda Shepherd was affected by anger in her turn. "How dare you speak to me in this fashion!" she cried. "You are addressing a woman of standing, in Lyddford. It is thanks to me that you are in the position which you so much enjoy. You have been lucky. It is not due to your own efforts that you find yourself living at South Court. I should be there, in your stead. It was my own actions which gave you this advantage over me."

So saying, Belinda turned and quit the garden. Both Lydia and I stood motionless, and watched her leave the premises by the hidden gate.

"What did she mean?" Lydia asked me. I saw that she had gone pale. Her anger had deserted her as swiftly as it had come. "I do not understand what she said. What did she imply? Of what was she speaking?"

I soothed Lydia as best I could. I put my arm around her and helped her back to the house. But Belinda Shepherd's words lived in my mind. And it seemed to me that we all stood on the edge of a chasm; or at the foot of a volcano. We were on the brink of some catastrophe we could not avoid.

The next day, I unfortunately suffered a return of the pain and stiffness in my head and shoulders. I knew that I had been up and about very early after the accident, in defiance of the doctor's orders. This was the penalty, I thought. I rested on the settee in the drawing-room, telling myself I should soon be recovered and about my usual pursuits again.

While I was immoblised, I found time

to consider the dominant emotions which now consumed me. My love for Harry Delaney filled me to overflowing, and appeared to gain in strength each day.

I longed to see him; if he called at the house to consult Edmund and our paths did not cross, I was desolated. Sometimes I thought he avoided me a little. Perhaps to ease his own pain, I told myself. Perhaps he too was desolated by the intensity of love.

But I could not be sure. I longed to know. I longed to know everything about the man I loved; his childhood, his manhood, his personal life.

I knew he had had a conventional upbringing with his sister in a clerical household in the country. He had joined Edmund's regiment, and had been zealous to attain his promotion by merit and not by preference.

The Prince of Wales had honoured him early in his career with an invitation to join the bodyguard. And now the Duke of Wellington had summoned him onto his personal staff. Harry Delaney was a man of repute and integrity, with a polished exterior but an inner spirit of fire and steel. I loved and admired him, and longed to know him better. Like all women in love, I yearned to know the secrets of my loved-one's heart.

While I was resting in the drawing-room Harry Delaney arrived at Charlecote with instructions to the chief of troopers, from the General. When this business had been attended to, he entered the drawing-room to pay his respects to myself.

"I am grieved to know that you are suffering again from the results of the Frenchman's attack," Harry said. He raised my hand to his lips in a formal salute, but his touch affected me deeply. I motioned to Harry to be seated, and he drew up a chair beside the settee. He appeared at ease, as if he had some unexpected free time at his disposal.

How I loved him, I thought, as I looked at the man before me. My eyes traced-out the shape of his head, with its black hair shining from its blue nimbus of light. His clear grey eyes, like water or crystal, were steadfast in their gaze. His mouth was stern but mobile. His body was lean and graceful, but alert as an unleashed steel coil. A good friend, but a desperate enemy, I thought. A man steadfast in his regard, and surely tender in love.

And suddenly, I longed to know of the recent events in his personal life, before I had entered it, and he had become the man I so secretly loved. What had taken place regarding Donna Isabella? Did he feel still the pain of his rejection? What of his plans for the future? I suddenly wanted to know.

Quite on an impulse I said, "Have you recovered from your travels in Spain? I know nothing of what you had to undergo, but I gained the impression that your course was a difficult one.

"And Donna Isabella," I went on. "I heard of your attachment, and its culmination. Am I forward to speak of this? If I am at fault please inform me, and I will apologise."

I thought I saw an expression of relief pass over Harry's face, as if he had longed to tell me of his ventures in Spain, and had never found the opportunity. "Friendly concern is never forward," he told me. "And as you translated so many of my despatches from the Spanish front,

I regard your enquiry as by no means out of place. Indeed, you shall hear what occurred in Spain. For the outcome of events there has had a profound and long-lasting effect upon my life."

He paused a little, and a breeze blew into the room, bringing with it the smell of grass, and trees, and the flowers in the borders at Charlecote. "My course in Spain was a complex one," he began. "For at that time I loved a Spanish lady, but Britain was then, and still is at war with Spain. There were naturally tensions and difficulties in our relationship. But in my unawareness, I thought that these could be overcome.

"Spain was my theatre of operation as an agent, as you well know, Caroline. I was therefore forced to seek an audience with Donna Isabella as an enemy of her country, not a friend. This inevitably caused her concern, and did not increase any affection she felt towards me.

"It is true, after my last leave in England, I returned to Spain hoping to ask the lady to be my wife. But other events intervened, and the proposal was never made.

"Donna Isabella was a lady-in-waiting to the new Spanish king Joseph Bonaparte, who was promoted by the Emperor Napoleon. She was jealous of her position and afraid of the future. She did not wish to lose her new-found security and her settled position at court.

"I was forced to attend this enemy court in disguise. Donna Isabella alone knew of my identity. Naturally, I trusted her. For I had come to bring her my protestation of affection, and to ask her to share my life."

Harry Delaney paused, as if reviewing the past and his own actions and those of Donna Isabella. He resumed:

"The Donna Isabella was a beautiful lady. Almost as tall as myself. Stately, yet with a sense of the incongruous. She had long dark hair and a white skin. She was much admired and courted by the Spanish nobility."

Harry paused again, as if marshalling his facts and the best way of expressing events. "I think I would not have pursued my suit with Donna Isabella with such force, had not obstacles been constantly placed in my way.

"The difficulty of seeing her, the impediment to winning her regard since I was an enemy national, the admiration of other men, and her own inexplicable nature . . . All these seemed to taunt me and to make my winning of the lady impossible. I pressed ahead with my pursuit, but sometimes I wondered about the worth of my goal."

Again he paused, and I guessed that this was not an easy recital for him. He was revealing so much that was deep and personal; while his whole life and training had schooled him to self-sufficiency and secrecy. I did not speak, but waited for him to go on.

"And now, you must remember the political climate in Spain at this time. You must recall that this country was in the grip of the Spanish Inquisition and the persecution of the protestants. Napoleon had supposedly suppressed the Inquisition, but believe me, its beliefs and practices remained in strong force during my time in Spain.

"Naturally, such persecution was alien to me, and to all Englishman fighting against Spain. The idea that the men and women should be hounded and persecuted because of their religious belief was an anathema to me. Particularly when this persecution was crowned with the Inquisition, during which bestial and inhuman tortures were inflicted upon innocent people, whose only offence was to differ in their expression of devotion to their God."

Harry halted again; clearly this was a matter upon which he felt keenly. He continued, "When I arrived at the Spanish court, during my last visit to Spain, I was anxious to see Donna Isabella, and I had brought her gifts with my avowment of love.

"But she would have none of the gifts, or hear any mention of my suit. She spoke only of the Inquisition, and the rightness of this cause. She recounted the tortures inflicted upon the victims, and described how they had recanted before they died.

"She appeared to glory in this recital, and her championship of these degrading practices nauseated me. I asked her to renounce her belief in the justice of the Spanish Inquisition, and this she refused to do. Indeed, she was indignant that I did not share her perverted joy in the horrors of this institution. Her unnatural pleasure shocked and horrified me, and at once, there was a difference of opinion and a quarrel. A quarrel that was bitter in the extreme, and which drove a division between us which it would be difficult to heal.

"In fact, there was no opportunity for our quarrel to be resolved. For so seriously did I regard this divergence of opinion, it was as if some scales were stripped from my eyes, and I saw the lady whom I had idealised in a different, and her true light.

"It is no exaggeration to say that, at this exact moment, my respect and my affection died. I saw Donna Isabella for what she truly was — a child of the Inquisition and a supporter of persecution — and I knew she was an alien being to me.

"I saw also myself for the first time. I had wasted my time and my life upon a chimera, upon service to a woman who was totally foreign to me. I had placed myself in an invidious position by my mistaken feelings. I knew I must quit the Spanish Court at once.

Harry fell silent again, and then resumed, "But I had reckoned without Donna Isabella. She also was distressed by our quarrel and the chasm which this had revealed between us. In her rage and fury, she told me to go. She then, without informing myself, betrayed me to the Spanish Guard.

"I learned later that she denounced me to the officials of the Inquisition as a heretic and a protestant. Armed guards were soon on my trail. I was forced to flee from Madrid into the countryside. I became a hunted man.

"In vain I tried to rid myself of my pursuers. I dared not contact any other agents or reveal myself to British sympathisers, for fear of reprisals. Protestants would have aided me, but I feared for their safety if I should be caught in their custody. I was finally cornered in Bilbao, taken by the guards of the Inquisition back to Madrid, and thrown into prison, there."

And now it was clear to me that the fact that Harry Delaney had been taken a prisoner by the guards of the Inquisition was a bitter event and a harsh recollection. He did not amplify this statement, but I guessed that the arrest had not been easy, and his capitulation enforced rather than surrendered. It was then, and is now, a grievous blow for a fighting man to be taken prisoner by an alien army. How much more bitter to be seized by guards of the Inquisition, when Harry abhorred so deeply their creed and their cruelty.

"I was locked in prison in Madrid in the vaults beneath the torture chambers of the Inquisition," Harry told me. "I, and other poor wretches imprisoned in these dungeons could hear naught but the screams of suffering from the dying. The sounds and sights and smells of that dire place haunt me still."

Harry fell silent again, and then continued, "After three nights, the door of my cell opened and my jailer entered. He told me that I was to be granted reprieve, and a safe passage to Cadiz.

"When I enquired as to why I was being spared the usual fate of this horrific place, he told me that I was being released on the intervention of a high personage, whose name he could not then reveal. He bade me get my bundle of clothing, and prepare to leave.

"In the corridors of these underground chambers the jailer told me that my release was propitious indeed. For I was due to be tortured that night, and killed on the morrow.

"At the door of the prison, a Spanish agent awaited me with disguise for two. Two horses were provided for us, to speed us on our way to the coast.

"When I enquired of my new protector as to the identity of his master, and who had arranged my deliverance from the prison and my escape, my companion answered dourly:

"You have been released on the intervention of the nephew of his Royal Highness, the Emperor Napoleon."

"He did not speak more, but he had said enough. I was dumbfounded, and quite beyond understanding, or any words."

★ ★ ★

"The nephew of the Emperor Napoleon!" I cried. I too was dumbfounded and bewildered. "Why should the nephew of the Emperor do this? What circumstances surround this rescue? Please tell me, Harry. I am almost too amazed to speak."

Harry laughed at my expression, and my words. I looked at his face; his expression had lightened instantly, and he was revealing his usual good humour and poise. I realised that this was the first time that Harry had smiled since he had begun his account of his misadventures. How I longed that always he should be happy, and should be smiling at me, thus!

"I met the Duke de Noilly before he was ennobled by his uncle, when he was a diplomat at the court of Spain, in Madrid. This was in happier times, before the enmity of our two countries soured relations both public and private, between our two peoples.

"We had many arguments upon philosophical problems, for he was a man of liberal views and good education. A liking sprang up between us. Then he was recalled by his uncle to Paris, and our friendship lapsed.

"I met the Duke again when I was at the court of Madrid, recently," Harry went on. "He was naturally guarded in his approach to me, since we were now theoretically enemies, and fighting on different sides.

"Yet we managed to meet, and resume our philosophical conversations. And I learned one aspect of the Duke's opinions which matched mine in its entirety. The Duke hated and abhorred the Spanish Inquisition and all its works and all it stood for. He loathed its oppression and bestial practices. This forged a bond between us, which I was to find circumstances did not break.

Harry paused again, and then continued thoughtfully, "The Duke de Noilly arranged my rescue, thus. He approached the King of Spain, and since the King had been elected by Napoleon, and held his power by consent of the Emperor, Napoleon's nephew was granted not only an audience, but immediate implementation of his request.

"The Duke de Noilly gave no reason

for his wish that I should be spared torture and death, save that of personal friendship. The Duke stressed, and I also believe this, that we were fighting on different sides, and were truly mortal enemies. But, he urged, the fate of one man could not affect future battles, particularly the fate of an undercover agent whose disguise was now openly revealed, and who could not in future with impunity return to Spain.

"Naturally, the Duke and the King placed a price on my head should I enter the Iberian peninsula again. This I have accepted, and this provision the Duke of Wellington accepted, also. I was glad to have my life and owe much to the Duke de Noilly. Yet I remain still his enemy, and he mine. That is understood between us, and will never be altered as long as this conflict lasts."

Harry fell silent again. Then he continued, "These circumstances had a profound effect upon my feelings and my life. My experience of the methods of the Spanish Inquisition, my imprisonment by their guards, my proximity to their torture chambers, all implanted in me one burning desire. A desire to prevent such an institution as the Inquisition from ever reaching our shores.

"I could not bear that our beloved country should ever be subject to such defamation, cruelty and disgrace. I determined then, and I am still of the same mind, to fight with all my strength to prevent a Spanish victory over Britain. No efforts are too great to prevent our country from being vanquished by men of this persuasion. Believe me, Caroline, I have devoted my life to this end. The winning of the war against all our enemies is now my prime concern."

I respected the deep and burning sincerity of Harry Delaney's words and feelings. That his was an intense and long-lasting conviction was plain. And I realised in that moment that he would give his life to uphold his aims.

★ ★ ★

It was at this moment that Mrs Bagehot entered the room with an infusion of tea for my headache; and a decanter of dry sack and a glass, for Harry. We took our refreshments gratefully. It was as if much had been expressed between us. We had passed a rubicon, and there was no going back.

"I honour your confidences," I said finally. "These shall be mine, and mine alone, as I know you would wish.

"I trust your service with the Duke of Wellington will be a long one," I added. "And that you will achieve all you have set out to do."

God keep you safe, I prayed secretly in my heart, but I schooled my face not to show any expression of doubt or concern.

Harry nodded his head, as if he understood much of my own feelings, without words. "I trust also that in future your feelings for the woman of your choice will be, happily, returned," I went on. "And that circumstances will be more propitious to your courtship, and your . . . "

I could not bring myself to say the word marriage. I thought I had said enough. I thought I had gone too far.

Harry Delaney bent over my hand, and

raised it to his lips. He murmured some words, as his lips brushed my palm. I thought he said, "I have found the lady of my choice, and love her with all my heart. But circumstances are not propitious, and we are riven apart."

The words were only whispered, and I could not be sure that I had heard aright. And indeed, it was as if the words were not intended to be a declaration or any expression of caring. They were uttered only to affirm an already accepted situation; they were uttered to accept an iron necessity of parting and renunciation.

It was as if Harry Delaney had accepted his fate of aloneness and separation. As I had accepted mine.

14

HARDLY had Harry gone, than I noticed the figure of Winifrede rushing past the windows on her way into the house. I wondered what the matter might be, for she had been obliging Lydia by doing some pressing and some fine needlework, which Lydia felt was beyond her at the present time. I had not long to wait, for Winifrede almost burst into the room.

"Lady Franklyn, ma'am," she began, "Mrs Hellier is . . . Something has happened, I do not know what, but Mrs Hellier is greatly affected, and . . . I fear she will collapse, or be overcome . . .

"Could you come to her at once, please? She begged me to fetch you to her side. In vain I told her you yourself were not well, but she did not seem to hear. If you could accompany me, I will attend you. I assure you the matter is not trivial, but deserves your presence at South Court."

At once I got up from the sofa, and drew around me my shawl. I dismissed Winifrede, after thanking her for her message, and her concern for both Mrs Hellier and myself. Something told me that indeed the matter was not trivial; and it was with a heavy heart that I stepped into the garden through the french windows, and made my way to South Court.

I found Lydia in her sitting-room; she sat on the settee quite still, her face ashen, her eyes shadowy and glazed. She might have been a figure carved from stone.

When she realised that I had entered the room, she raised one hand in a strange, hopeless, defenceless gesture. "She has been here," she said. "She came. I know now why."

"Who came?" I cried, for I felt deeply alarmed by Lydia's stillness and abstraction. "Of whom do you speak? And what did this woman want?"

"It was Belinda," said Lydia patiently, as if to a child: as if she expected me to know the identity of her caller. "Belinda Bagehot, as she was. Belinda Shepherd, now. Belinda came, and she brought with her, her little boy . . .

"I was surprised to see her after our altercation. I thought she had come to apologise for her spying and incivility. But it was not so. She halted on the front-door step and stood there . . . When I addressed her she did not speak or state her business. Indeed, she hesitated, as if she had lost her courage and her resolution. Then still without a word, she turned to go.

"But it was too late, Caroline. I saw. I knew. I understood. I saw her little boy, whom I had never seen before, and observed his resemblance to Philip . . . Caroline, George Shepherd is Philip's child. Philip is the father of Belinda's little boy. He seduced her, all that time ago, when she was a housemaid in Lady Deborah's house . . . I did not know. I had not an inkling of this truth. But I saw both the truth and the reality, now."

An overwhelming sensation of dismay and apprehension overcame me. What were Belinda's motives for this strange behaviour? To attempt to reveal the truth to Lydia, after all this time! And Lydia, what of the effect upon her? She sank back suddenly upon the cushions of the sofa, and lay like one dead; only the tears seeping from her closed eyes told me that she was alive.

At that moment, Winifrede arrived unbidden, and together we helped Lydia upstairs and put her to bed. I charged Winifrede to stay with Lydia while I returned to Charlecote; for it was now near to the evening supper-time, and Edmund would wish me to be in place. But at Charlecote, another surprise waited me. I found Belinda Shepherd sitting in the hall, awaiting my return.

I invited her into the drawing-room, and closed the door. I turned to face her. "Why did you behave as you did, Belinda?" I cried. "I am at a loss to understand your actions. Do you know how deeply you have distressed Mrs Hellier? I fear greatly for her health. To treat her so badly is inexplicable."

Belinda flushed, and we stood facing one another in the quiet room. "Please do not judge me without explanation, Lady Franklyn," Belinda replied. "There are other factors in this matter which you do not know, and of which I wish to apprize you, now.

"You will know that Philip Hellier seduced me while I was a housemaid at Charlecote," Belinda began. "He promised me marriage, and a place at Charlecote as his wife. And I longed for this. I longed to be a lady. I hated the life of a housemaid. You cannot know what it is like to be in service!" she cried. "I wanted to take my place in society as the wife of Philip Hellier, so that I could spit on those who scorned my humble beginnings. But he denied me this. He denied me my rights. And my pride would not allow the enforced marriage which Lady Deborah and the General proposed. But I swore to be revenged upon him, even if it took me the rest of my life.

"But after I had left Charlecote, and married Will Shepherd to give my son a name and a habitation, the force of my desire for revenge began to leave me. It was not until the engagement and marriage of Philip and Lydia Clements took place, that the strength of my feeling returned.

"For I knew then who had replaced me in Philip's affections. For I had known that almost instantly after my rejection by Philip, and my leaving Charlecote, he had become enamoured of another woman.

"Thus immediately he became engaged to Miss Lydia Clements, I realised that she was the woman who had supplanted me. Lydia Clements was the one who had taken Philip's attentions. It was Lydia Clements he had fallen in love with, after he had dismissed me."

I stared at Belinda aghast, remembering Philip's own onslaught upon my affections, my own innocent involvement in his life. But before I could speak to defend Lydia and reveal the truth, Belinda went on:

"So that, after their marriage, I blamed both Philip and Lydia Hellier equally for the reverses of my life. And I was determined to be revenged, in time, upon them both.

"Yet it is true, as time went on, again my resolution weakened. The kindliness of Will Shepherd my husband, the charm of my own son growing up, all seemed to take away the sting from my desire for revenge. It was almost from force of habit that I have recently walked in the shrubbery . . . And then, this afternoon, Mrs Hellier spoke to me harshly and ordered me from the grounds. It was instantly, at that moment, that my desire for retribution awoke afresh, and I determined that this time I would carry my action through."

Belinda paused, and I awaited for her to continue. My heart seemed to fail me at this recital; yet I guessed that there was more to come.

"I knew that Mrs Hellier was pregnant, so I . . . "

"Pregnant!" I cried. "Mrs Hellier pregnant?" I could not believe this was true; there were no signs, and I was sure Lydia would have told me of this.

"Mrs Hellier withdrew from society recently, and lived quietly and alone at South Court. In Lyddford, it is believed that she is expecting a child."

"So you went to her, at what you deemed her most vulnerable time, to . . . " To tell her the truth, I thought. To display unmistakably Philip's perfidy.

"I went with the intention of confronting

her," Belinda said. "I went to tell her the truth in words as it happened, the dates, the places, the times, everything. But at the very front-door of South Court I met a trooper on patrol who, knowing of my former friendship with Philip, told me the latest news. That Philip had been taken prisoner by the French.

"At once this news seemed to make nonsense of my desire and my intention. For Philip and Lydia Hellier would now encounter far more trouble than I could inflict upon them. All longing for revenge left me. My years of pain at betrayal and wish to avenge myself, passed away. I realised my good fortune in having Will Shepherd as my husband, and dear George as my son. And in having attained a respected position in Lyddford. I realised too, that we all face betrayal and disappointment at times, and must make the best of them. And so I moved to go."

And now Belinda paused, and then resumed, "But before I could leave the front-step the door opened, and Mrs Hellier appeared. She looked firstly at myself, and then at George. We neither of us spoke. Then I turned and led George away."

"But it was too late," I said. "Mrs Hellier had guessed the truth. You regretted your malicious intent; but the damage was done all the same."

A wave of weariness, almost exhaustion swept over me. How often does this take place in life, I thought. Regret at an action; yet the regret coming too late. The dreadful intent fulfilled in spite of the withdrawal. I shook my head.

"Leave me now, please Belinda," I said. "Do not approach Mrs Hellier again." I saw Edmund arriving at the house. With Belinda gone, sadly he confirmed that Philip had been taken a prisoner by Napoleon's forces.

"He was fighting a rearguard action at the Battle of Nations at Leipzig, and his platoon was surrounded. The men were killed, but the officers taken prisoner."

Edmund paused. "I believe it likely that his life will be spared. Obnoxious though it is to me to say it, Philip was a French agent, and I doubt that they will harm a traitorous Englishman who has served their cause."

With these bleak prognostications I had to be content. Edmund was outraged by Belinda's act of vengeance, but I begged him to take no steps in the matter. I thought enough harm had been done. I also asked Edmund that Lydia should not be informed of Philip's capture. To sustain further bad news when she was in so frail a state of health would be, I thought, more than she could bear.

It was later in the evening that Edmund clearly sought to lighten my depressed spirits. He said to me, "Have you noticed the difference in Harry lately, Caroline? I believe he is in love."

"In love!" I cried. I felt my heart begin to beat faster, my throat became constricted so that I could hardly speak. "What leads you to surmise this?" I faltered.

"I have observed his sudden change of mood," Edmund replied thoughtfully. "I have been pleased to see his happiness, following his dreadful experiences in Spain. I have been glad to note his pleasure in our life here. It is as if he considers some happy future of his own."

I did not answer and Edmund went on, "And then, another time, he is not so cheerful. He seems to be plunged into despair, as if he has encountered some obstacle to his love. Tell me, Caroline, I do not wish to pry, but . . . Has Harry given you any inkling of this new turn in his fortunes? Has he revealed to you who the lady of his choice might be?"

"Why no," I stammered. "Not at all. Truth to tell, I have not observed his moods, and . . . I am at a loss to . . . " My words died away, but Edmund did not appear to notice.

"One thing I am sure of," he resumed, "the lady in question will be a person of honour as well as beauty. Harry would never ask for less, in the choice of the lady upon whom to bestow his heart."

I felt the conversation was getting beyond my capacity to deal with; I rose to my feet with the murmured excuse that I must go to see how Lydia was progressing. As I passed his chair, Edmund took my hand and detained me briefly.

"Harry, as Deborah's brother, is like my own flesh and blood," he said to me. "I naturally feel interest in his future and concerns. If you should receive any indication as to where his affections are placed . . . Please inform me, Caroline. I long to know who is the lady of his choice."

I sped along the garden-path towards South Court. I found that Lydia was sleeping peacefully in her bed. But when I went to see her the next morning, I found that she was gone.

And news came through that day that the Duke of Wellington was expected at Charlecote in three days time.

15

EDMUND was now extremely busy with the arrangements for the visit of the Duke of Wellington to Charlecote. The twelve agents had to be alerted and given their instructions. Military security had to be strengthened for the visit to Lyddford of the British Commander-in-Chief. It seemed the perimeter of the house rang with military cries, and aides came frequently to the house on their urgent business with the General. But Edmund was not too busy to share my concern for, and aid me in my search for Lydia.

"I think it more than likely that Lydia has returned to Copthwaite Hall, as she did before," Edmund said. "I will send the carriage and a driver over to see what the situation is. Are all your preparations for the dinner for the Duke complete, Caroline?" he added. "I know you put matters in hand early, and I trust that all has gone well."

I thanked Edmund for this thought for Lydia, and continued, "Everything is in hand, and Will Shepherd has promised me his complete cooperation."

I had approached Will Shepherd earlier concerning the dinner for the Duke of Wellington. Naturally, no names were mentioned, but Will had promised to give the occasion his full attention to make this a memorable event.

Edmund had at first wished the troopers from the mess-hall at the barracks to wait at table and assist Mrs Bagehot and Winifrede where required. But I had remembered the dinner-party Lady Deborah had given, its glittering aura, its note of significance, and I had prevailed upon Edmund to allow me to engage civilian servers for this meal. I felt the dinner was my responsibility, and I wished to make the occasion an outstanding success.

"There will be fifteen at table, Caroline," Edmund told me. "The twelve agents, the equerry, the Duke and myself. The procedure is this:

"The agents will arrive at Charlecote at around five o'clock. At six o'clock the Duke of Wellington will arrive, and will then hold a military conclave with the agents. He will receive their reports personally, and inform them of their next assignment. He will tell them, I believe, of the next battle which will face the British, a battle upon which the Duke places total reliance for the winning of the war.

"At nine o'clock, Caroline, I ask that dinner shall be served. By this time the main business of the evening will be over, and I naturally wish that the subsequent occasion should be relaxed and pleasant. It will not be too convivial, for the Duke is not one to engage in wanton pleasure. But, of course, wines must be served, and I am anxious that these shall be of good quality and noble vintage. Does Will Shepherd know and appreciate this?"

"But of course, Edmund," I replied instantly. "Will Shepherd has promised that his wine-waiter, Bruce Finnegan, shall attend and give his whole attention to the condition and serving of the wines. I am sure there is no need to have concern over this matter."

Edmund smiled and agreed. "How

greatly I rely upon you, Caroline!" he complimented me. "I shall be truly proud to introduce you to the Duke as my wife."

He raised my hand to his lips and kissed my fingers. I smiled at him, honouring his kindliness, his integrity, his sense of justice and goodness. He was a man without parallel in the Duke's army, I thought. Only one other man matched him in stalwart qualities; and I put the memory of this man from my mind.

I went then to seek the coachman who had returned from Copthwaite Hall. Mr and Mrs Clements regretted, he said, that Mrs Hellier was not at her former home. She had not been in touch with her parents, and they did not know where she was.

Mrs Bagehot was drawn into the situation. "Mrs Hellier may have attempted to reach the coast, to try to find a ship that will take her to France. She may have decided to try to reach her husband. This is done now, ma'am," she added. "Some women pay large sums to seamen for this doubtful privilege. Many of these women are never seen again."

I hoped that this was not to be Lydia's fate. A small platoon of volunteers who were on manoeuvres around the coast and local roads were ordered by Edmund to keep a sharp look-out for the vanished lady. But the stalwart and invaluable volunteers, in their blue uniforms and white plumed helmets, reported no results. Lydia had vanished, it seemed, without trace.

The day sped swiftly by. Madame Serle delivered my new dress, for I had purchased a new gown in which to receive the Duke of Wellington at Charlecote. Mrs Bagehot and Winifrede sped about the kitchen and the house like homing birds. Yet I knew that everything was under control, and they were enjoying the special, though unknown occasion.

I went to see Will Shepherd at the Inn, the next day. This was the day before the Duke of Wellington arrived. Will Shepherd received me in his parlour. I was struck by the expression on his face.

"I cannot tell you how deeply I regret my wife's behaviour concerning

Mrs Hellier, ma'am," he said. "Belinda has been a wonderful wife and mother. I cannot speak too highly of her. Her lapse is inexplicable. I had quite thought her fit of girlish pique was over. She is sincerely grieved about the outcome of her foolish action. And now, I am faced with a difficult decision. A decision I must take alone, that will affect us all, and all our lives."

I saw his melancholy stance, his drawn and haggard face. The old Will Shepherd, so full of good humour was gone.

"I trust you will be able to attend the dinner at Charlecote," I said anxiously. "The General and I are relying upon your overseeing the whole event."

"I shall be there," he answered without enthusiasm. "I promised to attend before this matter with Belinda arose. I promised, and I will keep my word." But he sounded doubtful and defeated; and a small shadow of apprehension filled my mind.

I was worried too, on another score. Where was Gérard?

Gérard had vanished from sight of everyone at the barracks and Lyddford, when he had escaped from the jail. But he is somewhere, I thought. He is near. The shadow of Gérard lay like the shadow of the unknown over my final preparations for the momentous occasion of the visit of the Duke. But I did not mention my fears to anyone. They would have scoffed at me.

What could one discredited and hunted French agent do against the security machine of the British army? What were the fears of a woman against the certainties of soldiers trained to defend and disarm? I told myself not to be ridiculous, and tried to put my anxiety on this score from my mind.

Lydia was not heard of during that day; night fell, and she was still absent. I looked from my bedroom window at the surrounding scene.

It was now autumn. The weather, so enchanting until recently, had now broken. The air was dank and chill. Leaves were falling from the trees; the elm tree, part of so much that was significant at Charlecote, stood bowed and still. I shuddered. A desperate fear for Lydia filled my mind.

I could not sleep that night, and was up early the next morning. Edmund had already left for the barracks, for this was the long-expected day, the day of the visit of the Duke of Wellington to Charlecote. I prayed that all would go well; but could not still the turmoil of my thoughts. At last I took my cloak and left the house by the front-door.

The dank air met me in a wave, and I drew my cloak around me closer. I walked along the garden-path to South Court, and entered the still and lonely house.

It was now three days since Lydia had disappeared, and nothing had been heard of her; she had not been sighted, there was no clue as to her whereabouts. I walked through the house Lydia had loved so well, and to where she had come, after her marriage, with such high hopes. I was overwhelmed with sadness to think that these high ideals had come to naught.

In the sitting-room I paused. The arrangements of autumn flowers and foliage which she had loved to compose, stood forlorn and neglected. The silence was oppressive; gently, almost imperceptibly it began to rain.

I walked through the sitting-room at a loss as to my next move. I had come hoping to find some clue, some hint, some indication as to where Lydia had gone. We had been close friends. Surely there was something which would indicate to me, and me alone, her intention and her need? But there seemed to be nothing. I turned, dismayed and almost in despair, to go.

And then I saw her sketching-book. It lay open upon the bureau top. I looked at the uppermost drawing, and admired, as I always did, Lydia's skill and artistic sense. And then I stiffened. I looked more closely at the sketch. Was this the indication I was seeking? I asked myself. Was this the haven to which Lydia had fled in her need to escape, and find some private solace from her grief?

The drawing depicted the woodcutter's hut in Gartham Woods, nearby. I could see the roof, the logs which had been lashed together to construct the walls; the primitive window, the open door. Was this where Lydia had gone?

I did not wait to consider the matter or seek other help. If Lydia was indeed at the woodcutter's hut, then every moment was vital, in this inclement weather. I drew my cloak closer around me and ran from the house. I sought out the approach to the woods, and the long and narrow pathway which led deeper into the thickness of the plantation.

I had on only my houseshoes of soft leather; they were soon soaked, but I scarcely noticed. The rain fell steadily through the trees, branches caught at my cloak, but I sped on. Once I almost fell in the muddy and rutted track, but I recovered myself, and pressed forward to my goal.

And as I ran I remembered how often Lydia and I had walked along this pleasant path into the woods. In springtime, when snowdrops had wreathed the boles of the trees; in summer, when the blue of pheasant's eye had sprinkled the undergrowth with lightness; in winter, during the snow, when we had worn our overshoes and lined cloaks. But never as now. One of us, alone; seeking the other who had disappeared. I heard a distant roll of thunder, but I still ran on.

I reached the woodcutter's hut at last, and pushed open the door. A desperate sight met my eyes.

Lydia lay on a pile of sacks in one corner of the hut; rain had seeped in around her; the air was saturated with damp and cold. She moaned feebly when she saw me; she tried to raise herself, but I saw that any movement was quite beyond her. I gathered her into my arms and tried to reassure her in her grievous state.

Brilliant crimson spots of some malaise highlighted her cheeks and forehead. Her eyes were glittering with fever, yet glazed with incomprehension. She did not call my name, although she clung to me. She shivered uncontrollably as if burning; yet her hands and body were desperately cold.

I placed my cloak over her, and told her I would be back shortly. I ran from the hut, and back along the woodland path. The rain saturated my morning-dress; branches tore my hair from its combs. But I did not stop until I reached

Charlecote, and the lieutenant in charge of the troopers.

I told him what had occurred, and at once he despatched a corps of troopers into the woods to seek out Lydia in her improvised shelter. The six men returned shortly, bearing the now unconscious Lydia on a litter of entwined branches. They had laid over her their greatcoats, and one man had fashioned a kind of improvised canopy of boughs over her still and motionless head.

At Charlecote I had already alerted Mrs Bagehot and Winifrede. Mrs Sears was already on the premises, having come in to lend her aid in the kitchen. Mrs Sears took charge of Lydia, and the troopers carried her upstairs.

There was a pleasant spare room at the back of the house, charmingly furnished for visitors. It was in here that Lydia was lodged. She lay quite still and passive and accepted Mrs Sear's ministrations without demur. A fire had been lit; brass pans full of hot cinders had warmed the bed. Mrs Sears brought a hot toddy of rum, sugar and water; Lydia choked over the mixture, then drank deeply. She lay back upon her pillows in a sleep of abandonment and utter exhaustion.

All this had taken time, I realised. I stood on the landing in my saturated clothes, knowing that many of my tasks had been neglected. Mrs Bagehot brought me hot water in my bedroom, and I sponged my starved and aching limbs. I put on clean and dry clothes, and went downstairs.

The day passed swiftly. During the afternoon, several of the agents arrived. They took draughts of mulled ale, a cold collation of meats, and some of Winifrede's spiced cake and cheese. They assured us that this was much appreciated. Many had spent long tours of duty overseas; it was clear their service had been arduous and their relaxation of duty delayed. But they were in good spirits, and obviously appreciated the honour of the occasion; and the importance of their coming meeting with the Duke.

I was anxious to be changed by six o'clock, when the Duke was due to enter Charlecote. I remember I stood at the foot of the stairs, looking towards the upper landing. A wave of weariness swept over me.

It was at this moment that Mrs Bagehot came to me. I saw from her face that she had something of importance to impart.

"I am sorry to tell you, ma'am, that Will Shepherd will not be present this evening. He has sent a message that he feels such an occasion as your dinner-party is beyond him.

"You will know of the disaster which has overtaken him. He feels Belinda's action keenly. It is a kind of disgrace to him. He is considering selling the Inn, and leaving the town. Under the weight of this grave decision, he does not feel able to attend. I trust you will not be too disappointed and will understand his dilemma and his withdrawal, this evening."

"I am sorry," I said. "But is everything in hand? The other serving-men have arrived safely, have they not?" I asked Mrs Bagehot.

I reproached myself that I had not visited the kitchen during the past hours. I had spent much time with Lydia, and had been busy in the front of the house;

and knowing the expertise of the kitchen staff, I had not been worried about progress, there. But now I regretted that I had not somehow found time to see the serving-men. "Are they as they were at Lady Deborah's dinner-party?" I queried. "I shall have no fears, if they are the same."

"The same exactly, with one exception," Mrs Bagehot said. "Bruce Finnegan, the wine-waiter, has colic and is unable to attend. But he has sent his cousin, a personable young man called Tim O'Leary. An Irishman too from his name and accent, but willing and biddable and quiet in his way. He will pass, never fear, ma'am. And he will be under my own scrutiny until he passes the dining-room door."

I nodded, accepting her assurances without reservations. Then she went on, "But lawks, ma'am, the time is nearly upon us when the General will arrive with the guests. Hasten to change, ma'am, so that you can be ready to receive! I will send Winifrede to assist you. And she will bring the tongs to take the dampness out of your hair."

I smiled at Mrs Bagehot's concern, and went up the stairs. The vital moment passed; and the moment of danger; the moment when the course of history could be altered. But I saw no warning signs, and so went up to my bedroom to change.

Alone in the room, when Winifrede had gone, I allowed myself to savour the moment. Lady Deborah had always said that the hostess should enjoy her own party too; and in spite of everything I determined to try to to do this.

I looked at myself in the mirror. I saw that the damp had curled my hair naturally, and it hung loosely around my face in the tendrils of the time, with a coil at the back of my head, shining and smooth. My face was flushed from my exertions, and my eyes were bright now with anticipation. I held the rose-coloured brocade of my gown in my hands, and felt the gold thread which was interwoven with the silk. I hoped that Fate would continue to smile on me; or at least hold harm at bay during the coming days.

I tried to smile at my reflection in the

looking-glass. Though recent events had been unsettling and unnerving, I longed for the evening to outshine its portents. With all my heart I hoped that the dinner-party would reward us all with its own triumph and success.

16

THE Duke of Wellington arrived at Charlecote punctually at six o'clock. He was accompanied by Edmund, Harry Delaney and the Duke's equerry. I was not called upon to receive the Duke at this juncture; the agents and the Duke entered the study, and the door was locked and guarded by troopers. No sound of their discussions could be heard throughout the house.

I entered the dining-room to inspect the final arrangements. The white cloths, the silver service, the foliage in the centrepiece of the table, the wine on a side-table ready to be poured ... I felt pleased by the scene. I knew that the meal, in the kitchen, was approaching completion. I felt suddenly reassured that Charlecote would not disappoint the Duke; and our combined efforts would not cause Edmund a moment's question or doubt.

At this point a young serving-man

entered the room. He was Lance Pardoe, Will Shepherd's number two assistant. "I beg your pardon, my lady," he said when he saw me. He made as if to withdraw, but I stayed him. "What was your errand, Lance?" I asked him, and he replied, "Tim O'Leary, the new wine-waiter, is inexperienced in the serving of the wine. I have arranged that he shall decant the wine on the side-table, and I will pour it into the gentlemen's glasses. I could not bear to think that an inexperienced hand should make an error with the wine . . . " He stopped, his eyes wide, his expression dismayed. I tried to hide my smile at his seriousness; but remembering his trade as a potman, could not but approve of his gravity regarding his task.

I withdrew, and went to see Lydia. At just before nine o'clock the meeting in the study was over, and the gentlemen entered the drawing-room. And so, the moment which had been heralded for so long, was upon me. The Duke of Wellington advanced towards me, and smiling, took my hand.

I saw that the Duke of Wellington was a man of tall and slim build; he held himself erect, but without any suggestion of hauteur or presumption.

The gaze of his brown eyes was direct yet unrevealing; his features were well defined, almost bold in character; his nose was slightly hooked like a beak, his forehead and chin of definite shape and cast. His stance before me was courteous yet friendly; he was clearly used to polished company, as well as to conditions on the fields of battle which had been his life.

There was about him an air of solitariness; he was a loner, I was to discover later. He had the authority of character, he was a man who scorned the outward trappings of success. Yet he inspired me with instant confidence. I felt I could trust this man with my own life, and the lives of those whom I loved. I learned later, that his troops shared this feeling of confidence, and would obey his instant commands, whatever the consequences to themselves.

I curtsied to the Duke as he took my hand. As he bowed his head I saw that his hair was dark brown and well tended; he wore no wig. The agents also were wigless, following their leader's precept. I realised that the Duke was speaking to me.

"So this is the beautiful Lady Franklyn, of whom I have heard so much! My salutations, ma'am. It is indeed a pleasure to make your acquaintance. And thank you for allowing my men and myself to share your home. Come, let us be seated as we partake of some of your excellent wine. I find so few opportunities in my life to share my time with ladies as young and charming as yourself! Your health, ma'am!" And the Duke toasted me as he raised a glass of wine which he had accepted from the silver tray.

I noticed that Lance Pardoe was carrying the salver of wine around the room; Tim O'Leary had no doubt poured this in the dining-room. I thought the arrangement was working well. The agents had by now relaxed after their meeting with the Duke. Their voices rang through the room; their smiling faces augured well for the success of the rest of the occasion. I relaxed a little; it suddenly seemed that the evening was promising to be memorable and a credit to us all.

Yet I saw that Harry Delaney appeared unable to enter into the new spirit of the evening. His gaze as he watched me attend the Duke was sombre and preoccupied. I guessed that the session in the study had been a hard one, and much of moment had been discussed. I guessed also that Harry must support many of the Duke's commands. I did not doubt that his course was again to be severe.

Soon after nine o'clock the announcement came that the meal was served. As the agents stood aside, waiting for the Duke to precede them into the dining-room, I made as if to withdraw. But the Duke stayed me with a touch of his hand.

"But surely you will dine with us, Lady Franklyn?" he said. "I cannot believe that we shall be seated at this historic dinner without the company of one of our best translators! A translator upon whom several of our agents rely! Pray call for another place-setting, General," he told Edmund. "I would like to have the pleasure of your wife's company, and I request that she be seated at my right hand."

Edmund was clearly pleased by this mark of esteem, and directive. Another place was hastily laid at the table, and I entered the room on the arm of the Duke.

Before the meal began, Edmund called for a toast. "To the Duke of Wellington, upon whom our hopes of a British victory depend.

"Gentlemen, Napoleon is called the falcon by the French and Spanish forces. But the Duke of Wellington is the eagle! And the eagle will defeat the falcon, never fear. To victory, Gentlemen! And our Commander-in-Chief, the Duke of Wellington!"

We all drank our wine, as the Duke bowed his head in recognition. I was to learn later that the name bestowed upon the Duke by the British forces was indeed the eagle. And I saw from the strong cast of his features that he undeniably resembled this powerful and dominant bird.

And then the meal began. The soup was ladled from huge tureens; trout garnished with rosemary was served; capons were brought in, basted with butter and surrounded with legumes. A side of beef appeared. The wine flowed again. The scene was a brilliant one. The central lights from the ceiling of the room lit up the lavish table and the company; in the shadows the serving-men moved carefully about their tasks.

The serving-men wore brown breeches, with aprons of their trade; also white shirts with high neckcloths, rather concealing, and large powdered grey wigs. I noticed that Tim O'Leary, the novice wine-waiter, was a broad-shouldered young man with a spade-shaped dark beard which reached up into his wig. He attended to his task with the wine diligently, and, though he was difficult to see in the shadows of the room, I decided to commend his perseverance at the end of the meal.

The dinner was drawing to a close, the comfit of fruits had been served with soured cream and iced biscuits, when a strange incident occurred. Mrs Bagehot entered the room, and asked the General and myself to accompany her into the hall.

I knew some matter of importance

had come up, for naturally, Mrs Bagehot would not intrude into an important gathering of this nature without cause. Greatly mystified, Edmund and I accompanied her from the room. In the hall, an unexpected sight met our eyes.

Bruce Finnegan stood there, in a state of great distress. His clothing was torn and dishevelled, his face was bruised, dirty, and cut. He cried:

"I was not prevented from attending at Charlecote by colic, but I was attacked on my way to the house this afternoon! An unknown assailant overcame me, took my uniform which I carried in a leather bag, and after binding me, left me in a ditch.

"I feigned unconsciousness or even death, for I feared for my life from this villain's hands. That he had put paid to me he did not doubt. But I had to recover my wits and free myself, before I could hasten here.

"General Franklyn, you have an imposter here in your house, posing as a serving-man! I do not know his intention, but I believe it to be nefarious. Please hasten, sir, to . . . "

But Edmund had turned, and had flung open the big double doors of the dining-room. Bruce Finnegan, in the hallway, was visible to everyone in the room.

That something unprecedented had occurred, was clear to all present. The Duke of Wellington, his trained senses alert to danger, rose to his feet. But he was too late. His assailant moved towards him with speed and lethal intent.

At the sight of Bruce Finnegan, Tim O'Leary knew his deception was over and discovered. He seized from a holder within his shirt a knife, and lunged himself at the back of the Duke of Wellington.

But he did not reach the Duke. Another man interposed himself between the Duke and the assailant with the dagger. Harry Delaney stood, a living shield, before the Duke. Harry's arm went out as the knife fell; he twisted the arm which held the weapon, and the two men closed together. A struggle ensued, brief but bitter, violent and uncompromising; and then one man fell. The so-called Tim O'Leary dropped to the ground. Harry

Delaney stepped back.

Blood was streaming from his arm and shoulder; he would have fallen had not the Duke of Wellington steadied him. Both the Duke and Harry Delaney were stained by blood. They both looked at the assailant as he lay stretched on the floor.

The poniard had penetrated the young man's side. After a few moments of rictus, the young man lay in an attitude of sudden rest, after great conflict and exertion. His serving-man's wig had fallen off, revealing his auburn head. His black beard too, had been torn aside during the fray. His face lay unconcealed and strangely at peace, and vulnerable. His eyes, which I knew were blue, were closed for ever.

Harry Delaney knelt beside the dead man. His eyes searched the silent face. "Gérard Ramolino," he said slowly, wonderingly. "Duke de Noilly. Nephew of the Emperor Napoleon." And strangely and inexplicably, he began to weep.

My heart felt as if it was being torn asunder in my body. Gérard! Gérard the assailant, and he was now dead!

He was beyond all earthly help. And Harry Delaney in the throes of desperate emotion. I saw Harry keel over, even as he knelt by the side of Gérard. He lost consciousness, and lay beside Gérard as if he too had lost his last hold upon life.

I could contain myself no longer. I know that I ran across the room to where Harry lay. I knelt by his body. I gathered his head and shoulders into my arms. "Harry!" I heard my voice in a kind of soundless whisper. "Harry, my dearest, my beloved, return to me. I cannot bear it if you die . . . " Were the words uttered, or were they the unspoken echoes of my all-consuming emotion? "My dearest, I adore you beyond life, beyond death, beyond . . . "

I realised that there was intense silence in the room. I looked upwards and saw the intelligence agents and the Duke of Wellington framed by the brilliance of the lights, and crowded together in the shadows. Every eye was upon us, as I knelt with Harry in my arms. Yet I was beyond all circumspection and need for secrecy now. I bent my head and laid my lips upon Harry's hair. My tears fell, tears of supplication that he would live, and his life would be spared.

He recovered consciousness a little and stirred within my arms. "Caroline, my dearest," he said, and he drew my head down so that my face rested against his.

I raised my head at last, and looked towards the door of the room. Edmund stood there, as if petrified into stone. But he had seen, he understood, he had realised everything. I saw at first an expression of surprise, incredulity and astonishment upon his face. And then gradually, a deep and overwhelming despair overcame him. He turned away. But not before I had seen the hopelessness and desolation expressed upon his face.

★ ★ ★

The whole mêlée had taken only a few minutes of time; and now the other agents aided Harry, and Gérard's body was taken away. The Duke later commanded that his body be buried with full military honours. The nephew of the Emperor Napoleon deserved no less.

The evening came swiftly to a close.

Harry Delaney was taken to the military hospital at Lyddford Barracks. He had a wound in his right shoulder. The Duke of Wellington asked for and received concise explanations of the events which had led up to the attack on his life; he bade us farewell and returned to Lyddford Barracks.

At Charlecote, the meal was cleared, the servants dismissed, the lights turned out. I did not know it then, but the strategy for which was later to be the Battle of Waterloo had been discussed at my house. And the agents briefed in their tasks of reconnaisance, before the final and vital battles would begin.

No word was said between Edmund and myself concerning the personal events of the evening. But that Edmund now knew who the lady was whom Harry loved, was plain. And that I too, returned that love was obvious. During the next few days Edmund threw himself into his usual military pursuits; and I returned to my affairs concerning the household. Edmund visited Harry in hospital, and told me that he was progressing well.

Sadness and the heaviness of personal

grief filled my heart. Edmund's sorrow was hidden under preoccupation; mine was held in check. I guessed that Harry must face his own private unhappiness also, at the turn of events. It seemed that Fate and circumstances had brought us all nothing but the intensity of grief.

I awaited Harry's release from hospital, for I knew that he would visit me to say goodbye. This was our bounden duty, and must be our inclination. Even a conventional acquaintanceship would be impossible for us. I knew we must part, and remain severed for all time.

Two days before Harry returned to his military duties from the hospital, Edmund was recalled to active service overseas. His goodbye was tender and affectionate as always; for a few moments he hid his distress, and laughter and good humour shone in his eyes. I parted from him reluctantly. I longed for him to stay and for our former contented life to return. It seemed with his going that a chapter of my life was closing for ever.

Edmund was killed at the battle of Champaubert. His death appeared inexplicable, and without rational explanation. He was a General who equated safety for his men with the fulfilment of military objectives; he was known and trusted by his troops not to throw one life away. And yet . . . He himself entered a withering hail of gunshot from the French guns without protection or military flank movements. He entered a bombardment of gunshot, as if he was walking in the garden at Charlecote; relaxed, and without fear. He died, as he had lived, in integrity and prompted by the highest ideals of his life.

Harry came to see me upon a formal errand of condolence. The wound in his shoulder had almost healed, and he had recovered his health. We were both stricken by Edmund's death. For although we were innocent of any trangressions against Edmund or ourselves, the manner of Edmund's demise seemed to weigh insupportably upon us. We parted formally, and made no plans to meet again.

Matters were not made easier for us by our discovery that, in Edmund's will, he had bequeathed to me Charlecote, and half his estate. The other half of his money and possessions he had left to Harry.

By these means he seemed to give us his blessing upon our love and our possible future life together; yet still we remained apart. Edmund's action should have healed the suffering of his death within our hearts; yet neither gave the sign to the other to resume our friendship. It seemed we were in a stalemate of separation and despair.

Lydia recovered her health, but not her mental stability. Belinda Shepherd's abortive act of revenge and Lydia's subsequent ordeal in the woodcutter's hut, had unhinged her mind. She was taken to the Hospice of St Hilda, near to Maidstone, where she was tended with great devotion by the sisters. I visited her often, but she did not know me. She did not remember Philip, or any part of her past life.

She was not pregnant, though she had revealed to me at Charlecote that she had longed to bear Philip's child. She remained at the Hospice for many years.

Philip never returned to England. There was no trial and no court martial. Although he was a captive of the French at the material time, Philip was held responsible for Gérard Ramolino's death. The fact that the nephew of the Emperor Napoleon had met his death at Philip's home, was deemed sufficient to establish his guilt. Philip was executed without trial at the Prison of the Bastille. Lydia never knew of his death; and in her trance-like state, never enquired.

Will Shepherd, Belinda and little George emigrated to the Antipodes. This was their best course, Will considered, to enable Belinda to start afresh. For her action had been roundly condemned by everyone at Lyddford. For naturally, her misdemeanour became known, and the censure of all local people was severe.

I heard indirectly that Harry had been promoted by the Duke of Wellington to be head of intelligence in Edmund's place; the Duke had informed both Harry and Edmund, before Edmund's death, that he entirely understood the circumstances which had led up to Gérard's attack upon his life, and he held no person responsible. I did not doubt but that Harry would acquit himself well as the chief of the Duke's agents. He was no longer stationed at Lyddford Barracks; and of course, the study at Charlecote was now closed.

Many events had been crowding in upon us in England during these days. Napoleon's downfall, his sentence of exile to Elba, his escape. And time drew irrevocably near to Britain's final attempt to crush the would-be conqueror of Europe. The Battle of Waterloo loomed ahead.

I had lived quietly at Charlecote during this time, the life of a widow, and almost a recluse. Then one spring day I received an engraved card from the Duke of Wellington, asking me to attend a dinner-party at Apsley House.

So celebrated was the Duke now; so revered since his victories overseas that his simplest wish was like a command. For the Duke was acclaimed not only as a military hero, but as the creator of a new Britain; the liberator of our people into a new life. I deemed it impossible to refuse this invitation; and Madame

Serle was pressed into service with a new dress.

Upon my arrival at Apsley House, I was surprised to find this was a dinner-party for Lady Kitty, the Duke's wife, the Duke himself, and one other guest. And so I was not surprised when Harry Delaney entered the room.

He looked thinner, if this was possible, I thought; a little older, as we were all older, now. Yet he still had his old dynamism and poise. After the dinner the Duke took us aside.

"I wish to speak to you both upon a personal matter of importance, and charge you both to hear me out," the Duke began.

"I was privileged to be Edmund Franklyn's confidante while we were fighting side by side at Champaubert," the Duke told us. He fixed us with his penetrating brown eyes; eyes that could hold one spellbound, that brooked no denial or inattention. "He told me of his love for you both, and that it was his dearest wish that you should confess your love for one another, and be married.

"I entirely understand your feelings in

remaining apart," the Duke informed us. "But Edmund Franklyn would not have understood them, and would feel affronted that his wishes had not been obeyed.

"If your love has endured," the Duke continued, "and I believe it has, I charge you both to uphold the wishes of your benefactor. To do less than he desired would be, in my opinion, to dishonour his name.

"You are both guiltless of any offence against Edmund," the Duke went on. "You loved, but did not express or fulfil your attachment, or cause any harm. Indeed, Edmund told me of the love and joy you had both brought into his life. A love and joy he honoured and prized. His action gave you the opportunity to attain a devotion and happiness equal to his own. Indeed, Edmund expressed his thanks to you both by granting this gift of love between your two selves.

"I therefore, order you, Caroline and Harry, to think carefully over your present course, and to amend your ways. And if you decide to take my advice . . . And if you will care to set the date and invite Lady Kitty and myself to your marriage . . . I assure you we shall both be delighted to attend!"

After this conversation with the Duke, which affected us deeply, Harry and I naturally turned to one another again, with no shadow of hesitation between us. Our love had truly endured; indeed it had grown stronger and more intense by our separation. It was as if this time of being apart had allowed the events of our individual past lives to lose their poignancy. We had paused in our living after tumultuous happenings, before taking the most vital step of our lives, together.

We were married at Lyddford, and Charlecote became our home. Mrs Bagehot and Winifrede remained with us, trusted friends and companions. I treasured still the rose which Gérard had given me, in happier times; and Harry mourned the loss of the friend who had saved his life.

Harry and I attended the ball on the eve of the Battle of Waterloo as a married couple. Harry supported the Duke at the Battle of Waterloo, and returned to take his place on the Duke's staff when the Duke became Prime Minister of England. For after the victorious outcome of the Battle of Waterloo the flight of the falcon was halted for ever by the eagle's might; and the trappings of war were laid aside.

The love which Harry and I bore for one another blossomed with its own intensity, once we were free to express our affection. It was as if we held fast to one another and the treasures of our life, in case events should deny us again. But Fate was kind, and granted us the continuing fulfilment of our love. Love which had stood the test of time, adversity and denial. Love which blessed us both, our lives, our home, and our beloved family to come.

Other titles in the
Ulverscroft Large Print Series:

TO FIGHT THE WILD
Rod Ansell and Rachel Percy

Lost in uncharted Australian bush, Rod Ansell survived by hunting and trapping wild animals, improvising shelter and using all the bushman's skills he knew.

COROMANDEL
Pat Barr

India in the 1830s is a hot, uncomfortable place, where the East India Company still rules. Amelia and her new husband find themselves caught up in the animosities which seethe between the old order and the new.

THE SMALL PARTY
Lillian Beckwith

A frightening journey to safety begins for Ruth and her small party as their island is caught up in the dangers of armed insurrection.

THE WILDERNESS WALK
Sheila Bishop

Stifling unpleasant memories of a misbegotten romance in Cleave with Lord Francis Aubrey, Lavinia goes on holiday there with her sister. The two women are thrust into a romantic intrigue involving none other than Lord Francis.

THE RELUCTANT GUEST
Rosalind Brett

Ann Calvert went to spend a month on a South African farm with Theo Borland and his sister. They both proved to be different from her first idea of them, and there was Storr Peterson — the most disturbing man she had ever met.

ONE ENCHANTED SUMMER
Anne Tedlock Brooks

A tale of mystery and romance and a girl who found both during one enchanted summer.

CLOUD OVER MALVERTON
Nancy Buckingham

Dulcie soon realises that something is seriously wrong at Malverton, and when violence strikes she is horrified to find herself under suspicion of murder.

AFTER THOUGHTS
Max Bygraves

The Cockney entertainer tells stories of his East End childhood, of his RAF days, and his post-war showbusiness successes and friendships with fellow comedians.

MOONLIGHT
AND MARCH ROSES
D. Y. Cameron

Lynn's search to trace a missing girl takes her to Spain, where she meets Clive Hendon. While untangling the situation, she untangles her emotions and decides on her own future.